RYE FREE READING ROOM

FLOOD RELIEF 2007

Purchased with
Generous Community Support
After the Flood of 2007

Thank You!

Also by Claudia Mills

The
Totally
Made-up
Civil War
Diary
of Amanda
MacLeish

The

Totally Made-up

Civil War Diary

of Amanda MacLeish

CLAUDIA MILLS

FARRAR, STRAUS AND GIROUX   NEW YORK

Copyright © 2008 by Claudia Mills
All rights reserved
Distributed in Canada by Douglas & McIntyre Ltd.
Printed in the United States of America
Designed by Irene Metaxatos
First edition, 2008
10 9 8 7 6 5 4 3 2 1

www.fsgkidsbooks.com

Library of Congress Cataloging-in-Publication Data
Mills, Claudia.
    The totally made-up Civil War diary of Amanda MacLeish /
Claudia Mills.— 1st ed.
        p.   cm.
    Summary: While dealing with her parents' separation and her best
friend's distance, Amanda is able to work out some of her anxiety through
her fifth-grade project—writing a diary from the point of view of a ten-year-
old girl whose brothers fight on opposite sides in the Civil War.
    ISBN-13: 978-0-374-37696-3
    ISBN-10: 0-374-37696-4
    [1. Family problems—Fiction.   2. Diaries—Fiction.   3. United States—
History—Civil War, 1861–1865—Fiction.   4. Schools—Fiction.
5. Interpersonal relations—Fiction.   6. Family life—Maryland—Fiction.
7. Maryland—Fiction.]   I. Title.

PZ7.M63963Tot 2008
[Fic]—dc22
                                                              2007009162

For Rowan Bensko

The
Totally
Made-up
Civil War
Diary
of Amanda
MacLeish

1

Only in our house, thought Amanda MacLeish, could a Friday night family Monopoly game turn into the Civil War.

Friday night was family night, according to Amanda's mother. No sleepovers for Amanda and her best friend, Beth Gibson. No outings to the mall for Amanda's eighth-grade sister, Steffi. No real estate e-mails for their mom. No jazz radio for their dad. They could play a board game, or take a walk, or watch a movie, if they could all agree on the movie.

Now Amanda wished they had taken a walk. Or agreed on a movie. But these days her family was having a hard time agreeing about anything.

"Your turn," their dad said to Steffi.

Steffi picked up the dice. She had an infuriating way of rolling them, one at a time, jiggling each one in the palm of her hand for what felt like a whole minute before rolling it.

"Steffi, please," their mother said.

"I need a seven so I'll land on Reading Railroad. Then I'll own all four railroads. The computer always buys all the railroads."

With the first die, Steffi rolled a four. Then she jiggled the second die for an extra long time, as if that could make it roll a three.

She rolled a two.

"Great! Pay income tax." She glared at Amanda as if it were her fault.

Amanda tried not to notice. Reading Railroad was her own favorite property, but not because she liked owning railroads. When she was younger, she had thought it was pronounced *Reed*ing Railroad, like reading a book, not *Red*ding Railroad, like the color red. It still seemed magical to her—a railway that could carry you away to the land of books, with stops at Oz, Wonderland, Narnia, Green Gables.

"At Tanya's house, they have a family rule that nobody has to pay income tax or luxury tax," Steffi said.

"Well, we don't have that rule in our family," their dad said.

"*And* at Tanya's house, you get five hundred dollars for landing on Free Parking, and here you don't get anything."

"Just pay the tax," their mother said. From her tone of voice, it sounded as if she was mad at Steffi, but Amanda knew better. She was mad at their dad, who already owned Boardwalk and Park Place, which meant that he would win, even though Steffi claimed that when she played Monopoly against the computer, the computer beat her without having Boardwalk or Park Place or even any of the green properties.

"Your turn, Amanda," their dad said.

Amanda tossed down the dice quickly, as an example to Steffi. Unfortunately, she threw them down too hard and knocked over the lone, tiny green house her mother owned on Connecticut Avenue.

"Oops," Amanda said.

Without a word, her mother replaced the house carefully, lining it up precisely in the exact corner of the house row, as if it was really important to collect $40 in rent if somebody landed on it.

"Four," Amanda said. She assumed the roll still counted, even if it had caused a major housing calamity on Connecticut Avenue. "One, two, three, four."

Now *she* was on Reading Railroad.

"Go ahead, buy it," Steffi said. Amanda knew she meant, "Go ahead, ruin my chance of owning all four railroads, which is my new, best, computer-approved strategy for winning Monopoly."

"I don't want to," Amanda said. It wasn't Reading-a-Book Railroad. The only point in buying it, really, would be to spoil Steffi's monopoly on railroads, and Amanda wasn't in the mood for spoiling things any more than they were spoiled already.

"So you aren't even going to *try* to win?" Steffi demanded.

"I don't like owning railroads."

Amanda looked at the two deeds she had so far. All she owned were Mediterranean Avenue and St. Charles Place—two other great names for properties. "Mediterranean" made her think of pink, flower-covered villas set beside a bright blue sea. "St. Charles" sounded medieval, as if he might have been friends with King Arthur or Robin Hood.

St. Charles was probably the patron saint of something. Amanda hoped it was writing. She couldn't wait to have family night over with so she could go upstairs to her room and curl up in bed with her new notebook and start writing her first Civil War diary entry for Mr. Abrams.

It might be strange to want to do homework on a Friday night, but Mr. Abrams had thought up a great assignment. Every student in Amanda's fifth-grade class had been given the identity of some Civil War person, real or fictional, and had to spend a month writing that person's diary. Amanda was supposed to be ten-year-old Polly Mason from Frederick, Maryland, whose brothers were fighting against each other, one for the North and one for the South.

"So you aren't going to buy the railroad?" her father asked. At least when *he* asked a question, it was just a question.

Amanda shook her head. According to the rules, an unclaimed property was supposed to be auctioned off, but Amanda's family never played that way.

"Okay, my turn," her father said. He scooped up the dice

and shook them heartily in both cupped hands, then flung them down on the board with an eager grin. He always seemed to be expecting something wonderful to happen.

"Eight!" He drove his little car token across eight squares, giving one friendly toot as he passed their mother's top hat token.

Amanda giggled, but nobody else did. Steffi rolled her eyes. Their mother gave a tongue click of annoyance.

"Oh, boy!" He had landed on Marvin Gardens, the only yellow property he didn't yet own. His face lit up as he reached for his stack of hundred-dollar bills. He was always the one who got "LIFE INSURANCE MATURES—COLLECT $100" in Community Chest.

"One deed for Marvin Gardens," he said to Steffi. Steffi was the banker, to Amanda's enormous relief. Amanda hated it when people yelled at her for not being able to subtract 280 from 300 in her head.

"And wait a minute, I'll take three houses for them." He already had one house each on Boardwalk and Park Place.

Amanda's mother straightened her own house on Connecticut Avenue again. It had gotten crooked after the last exuberant dice roll.

"I'll take two more houses, too," she said stiffly.

But houses on the yellow properties were a lot scarier than houses on the light blue properties. Amanda wished her mother would land on the last unowned green property.

Then she'd have a real chance to win. It would be okay if her mother lost to her, or to Steffi. But Amanda didn't know what would happen if her mother lost to her father.

"Your turn," Amanda's father said to Amanda's mother.

"I know it's my turn."

She rolled the dice and landed on "GO TO JAIL." Amanda and Steffi used to make a big fuss if somebody had to go to jail. "Criminal!" they'd taunt. "What'd you do this time?" "Have fun in the slammer!" They didn't say anything now.

"Most wives and mothers I know think jail sounds pretty appealing," their mother said. "Peaceful, quiet cell. Three meals a day cooked by somebody else. Nobody else's jazz station turned up too loud. Nobody else's shirts to iron."

"I thought you had to make license plates," Steffi said. She had always been the braver sister.

"I'd like to make license plates. It sounds utterly mindless and straightforward. Put a rectangle of metal in the stamper. Stamp it. I could do that."

Going to jail had definitely put her in a better mood. Amanda liked jail, too, at least in the second half of a Monopoly game, when every move could land you on someone else's fabulously expensive space with a hotel. She always hoped she wouldn't roll the doubles that would open up the barred doors of the jail cell and let her go free.

In real life, she wouldn't mind jail if she could curl up on her bare little cot with a pad of paper and pen for writing. A book written by a ten-year-old from her jail cell was bound to get published. Maybe she could even publish her Civil War diary if it was good enough. There were always tons of historical diary books in the book fair at school.

The game went on. Steffi got the Chance card that said "TAKE A RIDE ON THE READING," so she finally got to buy it.

Amanda collected ten dollars from a Community Chest card for winning second prize in a beauty contest. Ha! The judges must have liked mousy brown hair, plain old brown eyes, and lots of brown freckles. Amanda planned to give Polly Mason, her Civil War character, long, golden curls and luminous blue eyes that reflected the cloudless blue sky above her rough-hewn log cabin.

Twice their father passed Go and put more houses on Park Place and Boardwalk. Their mother stayed peacefully in jail. Maybe the MacLeish family could play Monopoly after all.

Then their mother got out of jail.

Two turns later, Steffi landed on Park Place with three houses and had to pay $1,100.

"It's stupid to make some properties worth that much more than all the others," she said.

"That's life," their father replied cheerfully as he took her rent money and promptly bought two more houses with it.

"Monopoly is *not* like life," Steffi snapped. "In life you don't roll little numbered dice to find out what's going to happen to you. In life you don't draw little cards out of piles and do whatever the cards say to do."

"You have a point there," he agreed.

Steffi scowled. Amanda could tell she had been looking forward to an argument, but their dad never argued. His even temper was one of the things that drove their mother crazy.

Amanda landed on a railroad and had to pay $200 now that Steffi owned all four. Their father put hotels on Boardwalk and Park Place.

Their mother picked up the dice. She had reached her own Pacific Avenue. Amanda watched her nervously. If she rolled a six, she'd land on Park Place. If she rolled an eight, she'd land on Boardwalk. If she rolled anything else, she would be okay, though it would be slightly annoying to roll a seven and land on Luxury Tax.

Amanda wished she had a magic dice-rolling spell. "Not six, not eight," she beamed toward the dice, hidden in her mother's hand. Everything would be all right for the rest of their lives if her mother just didn't roll a six or an eight.

She rolled an eight.

Amanda's eyes met Steffi's. For the first time, Amanda knew that there was really something wrong with their family. In Beth's family, in normal families, it wasn't the end of the world if the mother landed on the father's Boardwalk with a hotel. In Beth's family, in normal families, the mother didn't say that she wished she were serving time in jail, and mean it.

Their mother moved her top hat eight squares to Boardwalk.

"Let's see . . . Boardwalk with hotel . . . That'll be two thousand dollars," said their father.

"I don't have two thousand dollars."

"You can mortgage your properties," their father suggested, as if he were a neutral financial counselor just trying to give helpful advice.

"You win." Her eyes glistened with tears. Amanda knew she wanted to say, "Just like you always win everything." But she didn't say it.

"Um—is family time, like, over?" Steffi asked hopefully.

Her mother was already putting the Community Chest and Chance cards back in the box.

Their father nodded. He didn't look happy anymore about winning. Further proof that Steffi was right: Monopoly wasn't like real life. You could win at Monopoly and still end up the loser.

Amanda hastily gathered up the property deeds, not bothering to put them in the proper order. She had a feeling her family wasn't going to be playing Monopoly together anytime soon. Then she fled upstairs, where a brand-new spiral notebook and freshly sharpened pencil were waiting.

April 2, 1861

Dear Diary,

Mother and Father gave you to me today for my tenth birthday present, and I am going to start writing in you right now. I hope we will become good friends. I will tell you everything. I wish

11

you could tell me things, too. It will be strange to have a friendship where one friend does all the talking and the other friend does all the listening. Though that's how I feel sometimes with my friend Betsy. She talks twice as much as I do. At school Master Taylor made her write on the blackboard one hundred times, "I will not talk to Polly."

I am Polly. My full name is Polly Jane Mason.

Because we are just getting to know each other, I will tell you some things about me. I have golden curls that take a long time to brush in the morning. Mother tells me I should not be vain about them, but sometimes I can't help it. I am so glad my hair is not mousy brown like Betsy's. My eyes are blue. I have no freckles at all. Mother is always telling me that if I don't wear my sunbonnet I'll get freckles, but I hardly ever remember to wear it and I don't have any freckles, anyway. Betsy wears her sunbonnet all the time, and she has more freckles than I can count.

There are five people in my family—five human people, plus one dog named Shep and two cats named Blackie and Whitie. Besides me, the other people are Mother, Father, Thomas, and Jeb.

Thomas is nineteen. He is so much older than I am that sometimes he forgets he is just a brother and tries to order me around as Mother and Father do. "Polly, go get the eggs from the barn." "Polly, go milk the cows." He treats me practically like a slave, which is strange, because Thomas thinks slavery is wrong and evil and an abomination in the eyes of the Lord.

Jeb is fifteen. He is a lot older than I am, too, but he still likes to go sledding with me in the winter and catch fireflies with me in the summer. He says that slavery is not so bad. He says most slaves couldn't take care of themselves if they didn't have owners to look after them. Jeb says the North shouldn't tell the South it can't have slaves. The one thing Jeb hates most in the world is if anybody tells him what to do, especially Thomas. He and Thomas fight all the time.

I agree with Thomas that slavery is wrong. How could it be right for one human being to own another human being? But I agree with Jeb that the North shouldn't tell the South what to do. It's confusing to agree with both brothers when they never agree with each other.

I love both my brothers, but down deep I love Jeb more. Is that a terrible thing to say, dear Diary? You must promise not to tell anybody else the secrets I tell you!

The South has seceded now and wants to be its own country, called the Confederacy. Part of me thinks that's okay. Why shouldn't it be separate if it wants to? But part of me feels sad. A country is kind of like a family. Even if you don't agree about things, you should still stay together.

I hope that Mother and Father and Thomas and Jeb and Shep and Blackie and Whitie and I will be together forever.

2

"*Is anyone willing to share his or her first* diary entry?" Mr. Abrams asked the class Monday morning. They were all seated cross-legged on the brightly patterned carpet by his comfy-looking rocker in their classroom gathering place.

Sitting next to Amanda, Beth shook her head emphatically. "Mine is terrible!" she whispered to Amanda. "I'm supposed to be the wife of a Confederate soldier who dies in the Battle of Bull Run. But I can't think of anything for my characters to say that doesn't sound lovey-dovey and stupid. 'I hope you don't die in battle, my darling!' 'I hope so, too, my love!' "

Amanda giggled, even as she felt a stab of pity for the young wife, soon to be a young widow. Maybe with a baby on the way, a son, never to know his brave soldier father.

"Anybody?" Mr. Abrams asked gently, after a long pause.

Amanda felt his eyes on her. He knew how much she

loved to write. Usually Amanda was the first to volunteer to share her poems and stories. That was part of the point of writing them, so that somebody else could read them and think, *Yes! I've felt that way, too.* But her diary entry felt so private. Hadn't Polly explicitly told her diary never to reveal the secrets written there? Would Polly want Amanda's whole fifth-grade class to know that she loved her brother Jeb more than she loved her brother Thomas?

Of course, Polly and Jeb and Thomas weren't real, Amanda reminded herself. It wasn't wrong to betray the innermost secrets of made-up people, was it?

She wasn't willing to raise her hand, but she gave a tiny nod, and Mr. Abrams's middle-aged face creased into a grateful smile.

"Amanda! Thank you! All right, everybody," he said to the rest of the class, looking directly at Ricky and Lance, who had started a thumb-wrestling match over in the corner. "Let's all listen to Amanda's diary entry."

Ricky's thumb came down triumphantly on Lance's. Lance gave Ricky a half-congratulatory, half-retaliatory whack on the shoulder. Then the boys turned toward Amanda. The kids in the class usually did what Mr. Abrams said. He expected everyone to be kind and courteous, so even kids like Ricky and Lance tried to act that way.

Amanda felt shy as she started to read, in a low, clear voice, but when she read the line about Betsy's freckles, the others laughed. *They like it,* she thought. As she read aloud about Jeb and Thomas, they seemed even more real to her than when she was writing about them.

" 'I hope that Mother and Father and Thomas and Jeb and Shep and Blackie and Whitie and I will be together forever.' "

Beth started clapping, and then everyone else was clapping, too.

"Amanda, that was wonderful!" Behind his thick glasses, Mr. Abrams's eyes shone. "Class, what did you like best about Amanda's diary?"

"I liked everything!" Ricky said.

Amanda knew he said it because it was easier to say you liked the whole thing than to think hard enough to pick out one specific feature that worked especially well. Still, it was pleasant to get such an enthusiastic comment.

James raised his hand.

"James, what did you like?" Mr. Abrams asked.

Oh, no. James was the only African American kid in the class. Suddenly Amanda wasn't sure she should have made Polly say that Jeb thought slaves weren't smart enough to take care of themselves without a master. Maybe James would think *she* thought that black people weren't as smart as white people. She hoped he knew that she, Amanda, didn't think all the same things that Jeb, or even Polly, did.

"I liked the way she made her favorite brother have the bad views on slavery, and the other brother have the good views. You'd expect the opposite, so that made it interesting."

16

"Yes! That's a great comment, James. When we read about history, we tend to assume that all the good people thought exactly the way we do today, and only the bad people held views we now find repugnant. But that's not true, is it? And Amanda showed us that in her diary. Good for you, Amanda, and good for you, James, for noticing."

Amanda smiled at James, and he smiled back.

"Who else would like to read?" Mr. Abrams asked.

Now lots of hands were in the air. Mr. Abrams called on Meghan, a perky blond girl who took Irish dancing lessons with Beth. Meghan's Civil War character was a Northern girl Polly's age who helped slaves escape on the Underground Railroad. Meghan's entry was well written, though her Martha character somehow didn't feel as real as Amanda's Polly. But maybe to Meghan, Polly didn't feel as real as Martha.

Beth gave the compliment this time. "I liked how you described all the smells in the barn where the slaves were going to be hiding."

Amanda agreed. She'd have to make sure that Polly described a lot of smells.

The next reading was by Patrick, who was supposed to be a thirteen-year-old who ran away to join the Union army as a drummer boy.

"I am Johnny . . . Johnny . . ." Patrick squinted at his handwriting. "I can't read my last name. Johnny . . . What's my last name?" he asked Mr. Abrams.

"McTaggart," Mr. Abrams said.

"And I live in . . ." Patrick studied his scribbled sheet of paper again. "It starts with *M*."

"Massachusetts." Mr. Abrams helped him again.

Ricky started to laugh, but a look from Mr. Abrams stopped him.

Amanda tried to listen, but every time Patrick paused to decipher another word, she was back at home reliving the weekend. Things hadn't gotten any better after the Friday night Monopoly game. Well, Saturday had been better, but only because her mother was gone all day showing houses to her real estate clients. Her father was out most of the afternoon, too, taking a jazz improvisation class he had won in a silent auction at Steffi's school. But then he went out for drinks with some of the people in his class, and came home late, and missed dinner. Amanda's mother threw the leftovers down the disposal instead of just putting them in a plastic container in the fridge.

Sunday they had all been home, but her parents weren't speaking. Once, Amanda had gone with Beth's family to a Quaker church service, where people sat together in silence for a whole entire hour, and the silence there was hopeful and holy. The silence at Amanda's house was horrible. Never before had Amanda realized that there were so many different kinds of silence.

Patrick finished reading. The class clapped politely.

"What did you like about Patrick's diary entry?" Mr. Abrams asked.

What could anyone possibly say? "I liked the places where you could read your own handwriting." But no one would want to say something mean in Mr. Abrams's class.

Beth raised her hand again, as Amanda had guessed she would. Beth was always willing to be kind. "You gave us lots of details about everyone in your family."

Too many, Amanda thought. The reader didn't need to know every single person's height, weight, birthday, and favorite color.

"I liked everything!" Ricky said, and the class laughed, but in a friendly way.

Lance read his next. "I'm supposed to be black," he explained. "I'm a slave boy in South Carolina. So that means I can't read and write so good. Okay, here's my diary. 'Deer Diary'—I misspelled *dear* to make it *d-e-e-r*. 'I am a slav boy'—I left the *e* off *slave*. 'I picks cotton all day long. I gets tired of pickin' it. My massah, he beats me sometimes coz I don't pick it fast enough. I sho hate bein' a slave. The end.'"

Amanda didn't know if she should clap or not. Was Lance making fun of the slave boy for his poor grammar and spelling? How well would Lance be able to spell if he had been a slave, picking cotton all day long? Slaves weren't even allowed to learn how to read or write.

She could hardly bear to look at James, but when she did, she saw that he was clapping with the others. And when Mr. Abrams asked what people liked about Lance's diary, James was the first to raise his hand.

"I liked how Lance tried to show what a slave boy back then would really sound like. He didn't make him sound like people sound today."

The tense knot inside Amanda's stomach relaxed. At least, one tense knot did. Maybe Lance's diary wasn't racist, after all, if James liked it.

"Good observation, James," Mr. Abrams said. Amanda couldn't tell if he was relieved, too.

And she still wondered what James, deep down, was really thinking.

★ ★ ★

Amanda walked home alone from school; Beth had a dentist's appointment. Maybe Amanda's mother would be home; maybe she would be out showing houses. Her father would be at his architect's office until almost seven. Steffi would be over at Tanya's house.

If Beth hadn't had a dentist's appointment, or Irish dancing class with Meghan, Amanda would have been at Beth's house. Silence was never scary at Beth's, where Beth's mother would be baking bread from her own hand-ground flour, while her father wrote his books on how to live an environmentally sustainable lifestyle. Beth's family didn't even play Monopoly. Beth's father said he didn't see why it was fun to ruin and bankrupt everyone you knew while becoming a filthy-rich real estate tycoon and developer.

The front door was unlocked. Amanda's mother must be at home. Amanda hoped that was okay. But as soon as she came into the kitchen and saw her mother sitting at the kitchen table, she knew it wasn't okay. Her mother was crying. Her eyes were red and streaming, and a pile of balled-up, soggy-looking tissues was on the table in front of her.

"Oh, honey, I thought you were going to be at Beth's. I didn't mean for you to see me this way."

As if to pull herself together, her mother stood up and faced the window. Amanda didn't want to ask, "What's wrong? Why are you crying?" She was afraid to hear the answer.

Then her mother turned toward her again. "I was going to wait until Steffi was here, too, and tell both of you together. But now that— I guess there's no point in waiting. Amanda, your father left."

"Left?" Amanda repeated stupidly.

"He's moved out."

Amanda couldn't believe it. How could her gentle, good-natured dad get mad enough over anything to pack up and *leave*, walk out, abandon her and Steffi? It was impossible. She could have imagined her mother leaving, making a scene, stalking off in a rage, but not her father. For a second she thought of him driving away in the little Monopoly car, toot-tooting merrily in farewell. None of it made any sense.

"Why?" she made herself ask.

Amanda's mother lifted her chin. "Because I told him to."

Amanda just stared at her mother, too stunned to speak. If that was true, she didn't think she could forgive her mother, ever.

April 23, 1861

Dear Diary,

Something terrible has happened. The Rebels fired on Fort Sumter, a Union fort in South Carolina. Now the North is going to war with the South. War! Soldiers from the North and soldiers from the South will be fighting each other, shooting each other with rifles and cannons, trying to kill each other.

Thomas has already enlisted for the North. He saddled up our horse this morning and rode off into town and then rode home to tell us. Mother threw her apron over her face and started crying. Father turned very pale, but he strode across the room and shook Thomas's hand, and I knew that Father approved. I couldn't cry or shake his hand or anything. I'm too angry at Thomas for doing this. He's the one who's always telling me not to be rash and impulsive. "Think first, Polly!" "Count ten before you speak!" "Look before you leap!" But he didn't think first, or count ten, this time. I don't think you can un-enlist, go back to the generals and tell them that you've changed your mind, that you just remembered that it's only April and your father needs you to help with the farm. And your little sister needs you, too. Just because she does.

I know you're wondering how Jeb took the news. Jeb wasn't there when Thomas told us. He's off in town, but he walked there, six miles each way, because Thomas had Nell, the horse. I'm glad he's too young to enlist. Fifteen has to be too young. I know some boys even younger than that are going as drummer boys. But Jeb wouldn't want to be a drummer boy. He'd want to fight for the South, not bang a drum for it.

Wait. From my window I see him walking up the road.

Diary, he did it. When I ran down the road to meet him, he said, "Give me a hug, Polly. I'm a soldier now." His eyes were extra bright when he said it, mostly with excitement, I guess, but maybe with some fear, also.

"You're too young," I told him.

Jeb laughed. "I look eighteen, don't I?"

I shook my head. He looks lots younger than Thomas, even if he's taller now. He's so skinny, and his hair sticks up like a little boy's hair, and his teeth still look too big for the rest of his face. The tears I hadn't cried over Thomas started to run down my cheeks.

"Aw, come on, Polly! The war's going to be over after the first battle, everybody says. The South is going to whup the North so bad they'll be sorry they ever messed with us."

Us? Since when was Jeb a Southerner? Maryland was still part of the Union, even if lots of folks here thought the same way Jeb did.

"Polly, if I don't go now, it'll be over before I get there, and I'll miss all the fun."

That was too much. "War isn't fun!" I shouted. He may be fifteen while I'm only ten, but it's plain I know more about war than he does.

"Thomas has enlisted," I blurted out. I didn't need to tell him for which side.

His face darkened. "I figured he would."

"Are you going to say goodbye to him?"

"There's nothing to say."

But the next morning, before dawn, when Thomas was preparing to leave, and Mother and Father and I were all hugging him, and crying, Father crying, too, I heard Jeb stirring in his room upstairs. And when Thomas started down the road alone, on foot this time, nobody but me saw Jeb slip out the back door and race down the road after him, and they grabbed each other in one long, hard hug.

Oh, Diary, I'm weeping now for my poor brothers, fighting each other.

But even more, dear Diary, I'm weeping for myself.

3

Amanda didn't want to go downstairs for dinner. She wanted to stay in her room being Polly Mason whose parents were still living together in the same log cabin instead of Amanda MacLeish whose parents were—separated, she guessed. That's what it was called when one parent moved out. Separated, not divorced. Did most separated people get divorced? Or did most separated people get unseparated? Like a broken plate with the two halves glued back together again, so that you could barely see where the plate had cracked.

Amanda heard a knock on her door, and then Steffi pushed it open. "Mom told you?" Steffi asked from the doorway.

Amanda nodded. Steffi plopped herself down on Amanda's bed. Amanda swiveled around in her desk chair to face her. Steffi didn't look upset, but it was often hard for Amanda to know what Steffi was thinking; her sister could be kind and caring one minute, and then sarcastic and almost nasty the next.

"You saw it coming, didn't you?" Steffi asked.

Had Amanda seen it coming? "Maybe. I mean, I knew they were fighting. But lots of people fight."

Beth's parents didn't fight.

"Lots of people get divorced, too," Steffi said. "Half of all marriages end in divorce."

"Not in my class at school," Amanda pointed out. "Hardly any of the kids at school have divorced parents." Just Lance, and two or three other kids.

"Maybe some of those marriages are second marriages. The parents already had their divorce, with somebody else." Steffi sounded so matter-of-fact, the way she said "had their divorce," as if everyone was going to get one, and it was just a question of when. But even if half of all marriages ended in divorce, that still meant that half of all marriages *didn't*.

"Do most people who separate end up getting divorced?" Amanda asked, since Steffi seemed to know so much about divorce.

"Uh-huh. Like movie stars. First you hear that they had a press conference announcing they're getting separated from some other movie star. Then you hear that they're dating some new movie star they met while filming their next movie on location somewhere. Then you hear that they're divorced from the first movie star and married to the second one."

"You never hear that they've gotten back together with the first movie star?"

Steffi thought for a moment. "Well, sometimes they do. But they usually get married to other people in between."

Amanda was tempted to say that movie stars might not be the best example of typical married people, but she didn't want to make Steffi mad. What she really wanted was to ask Steffi whether she thought *their* parents would get back together, but she was afraid Steffi would say, "Oh, they're probably going to get their divorce over with now," in that bright, careless, know-it-all tone, as if it didn't matter all that much whether the MacLeishes were in the half that stayed together or the half that fell apart.

"Did Tanya's parents get separated first before they got divorced?" Amanda asked instead.

Tanya's parents had gotten divorced a long time ago. They had both remarried, so Tanya lived with her mother and stepfather and half sister here in Maryland, while her father lived with his new wife and Tanya's two half brothers in California.

"Probably. Tanya likes going to see her dad in California. She says the boys in California are cuter. Or she used to say that until she started liking Mike Weil."

"There's always some boy that Tanya likes."

"Yeah, but Mike Weil likes her back. He's okay, I guess, for an eighth-grade boy. You know how one dog year is equal to seven human years? Well, thirteen years for a boy is equal to ten years for a girl. I'm not kidding. Half the boys in my class even look like they're ten."

Amanda didn't want to talk about the maturity levels of eighth-grade boys versus eighth-grade girls. "Doesn't Tanya miss her dad the rest of the time?"

Steffi shrugged. "She deals with it."

Maybe once your parents had their divorce, that was all you could do: deal with it.

★ ★ ★

Dinner was surprisingly normal—the food at least: chicken with lemon and basil, wild rice, a green salad. Often their father worked late, so Amanda, Steffi, and their mother ate without him. Now his empty chair looked emptier, deserted, forlorn, as if it knew it was going to be empty forever.

No! Amanda wasn't going to start crying, she wasn't.

"How was school?" her mother asked after her first few bites of chicken.

"Mom!" Steffi snapped. "We're not exactly sitting here thinking about *school*."

So Steffi hadn't shrugged off the news as if it were just one more movie star's predivorce press conference.

Emboldened by Steffi's comment, Amanda made herself ask, in a small voice, "Where did Daddy go? Where is he now?"

"He's staying at a motel until he can find an apartment."
Their mother's voice was smooth, calm, revealing nothing.

"Which one?" Amanda asked.

Why couldn't he just live at home while he was looking for an apartment? Why did he have to look for an apartment at all?

Their mother seemed impatient now. "The Best Western north of town."

Amanda tried to remember if she had ever seen it. She had never thought to check out the locations of the various local motels in case her father might someday be living in one.

"With the heated pool out front?" Steffi asked. She sounded ready to go swimming, to pack up her swimsuit and goggles and sunscreen and head over to Dad's for a mellow late-summer dip.

Their mother nodded.

"Can we see him?" Amanda asked.

Lance spent every other weekend with his dad. It had been Lance's favorite excuse, last year in fourth grade, for why he didn't have his homework to turn in: "I left it at my dad's house." Fleetingly, Amanda imagined herself lying on a chaise longue by the Best Western pool, writing in her Civil War diary.

"Nobody's stopping you," her mother said. Then, apparently regretting her flippant tone, she laid down her fork.

"Girls, I know this isn't the way parents are supposed to

do it. We're supposed to sit down with you together and explain everything. That we both love you, that this isn't your fault, that we're going to try to make the transition as painless as we can for you. And we *do* love you, and it *isn't* your fault. But your father and I can't have that big talk with you right now. I don't know how any parents can do that. If you can get along well enough to have that kind of conversation, you probably don't need to have the conversation in the first place."

How come everyone else in Amanda's family knew so much about divorce? Had her mother been reading up on the topic? The ideal conversation sounded horrible to Amanda, the way her mother had described it, false and scripted, a prepared speech that people could recite without meaning a word of it. But at least if her family were having that ideal conversation, her father would be here now, and Amanda could look into his eyes and try to figure out if he wanted to leave, or if his leaving was all Amanda's mother's idea.

On the other hand, if he had been there, giving her a meant-to-be reassuring grin, Amanda wouldn't have been able to keep from crying.

"He said he'd call you. At eight o'clock tonight."

"I already told Tanya I was coming over to do homework," Steffi protested.

Amanda knew Steffi and Tanya weren't going to be doing homework. They were going to listen to music and analyze every sentence spoken to Tanya by Mike Weil. Amanda couldn't believe that Steffi would choose an evening doing that over talking to their dad, when he was sitting all alone in some barren motel room, probably listening to happy families splashing in the heated pool outside his window.

Her face must have shown what she was thinking, because Steffi shot her a defensive glance. "It's not like I'll never be able to talk to him again."

"That's all right," their mother said. "Amanda, you can be the one to talk to him tonight."

Amanda wondered if Steffi was going to tell Tanya what had happened. Maybe Tanya would think it was a relief to get your parents' divorce over with.

But Amanda would never feel that way. She wasn't going to tell Beth, she wasn't going to tell anyone, she wasn't going to "deal with it." She was just going to wish as hard as she could that it weren't really true.

The phone rang exactly at eight. On the first ring, Amanda snatched it up. "Hello?"

"Hi, Mandy," her father said. He was the only one who called her Mandy.

"Hi, Daddy." She still thought of him as Daddy, not Dad, even though she knew it sounded babyish.

There was a pause.

"I'm sorry, honey." His voice was quiet, sad, not like his usual voice at all.

"I'm sorry, too."

"I didn't want this to happen."

Then don't let it happen! Make it un-happen. Come back home again. But he couldn't come home, not if her mother didn't want him there.

"I love you, you know that, don't you? This has nothing to do with you and Steffi."

It sounded just like the ideal conversation, but Amanda didn't think he was quoting lines he had read in a book.

"I know."

Another long pause.

"Are you and Mom going to get a divorce?" She knew now, from Steffi, that it was fifty-fifty. She could picture Steffi rolling the Monopoly dice, one die at a time, to make the outcome what she most wanted it to be.

"I don't know," he said.

There was an awkward silence. Amanda couldn't think of anything else to say. She didn't think her father could think of anything else to say, either.

"Is Steffi around?"

"She's at Tanya's."

"Tell her I love her, okay?" He didn't sound mad that Steffi wasn't there.

"Okay."

"And I love you, Mandy."

"I love you, too, Daddy."

Then she hung up the phone.

May 15, 1861

Dear Diary,

It's good I have you to write to. Thomas is gone. Jeb is gone. Jeb left the morning after Thomas did.

"Who's going to help me with the crops?" Father asked Jeb. Father hadn't asked that of Thomas when Thomas said his good-byes.

Jeb didn't look sorry. "Polly here'll help you, right, Polly?" He grinned at me.

"No," I said, refusing to give him my permission to leave us all behind. In truth, I wanted to work outdoors, feeling the warm sun on my hair and smelling the freshly plowed earth. But not if it made it easier for Jeb to go.

He kissed me anyway, and kissed Mother, and shook hands with Father. And then he was off to join his regiment.

The house is awful quiet without them. Three people aren't enough for a cabin made for five. The kitchen floor is so clean without their big old boots tracking in mud after every rain. I hate to look at it. Shep still keeps watch by the front gate, waiting for them to come home. Blackie leaps into my lap as soon as I sit down. She always liked Thomas best, but now I'm the sudden favorite. Whitie dragged in a dead bird as a present to cheer us up, but it didn't cheer me up at all. With Jeb gone, I was the one who had to pick up that stinky, rotten thing and throw it back by the pigpen.

At school, I haven't told Betsy yet that Jeb is gone. She knows about Thomas, but I can't make myself tell her about Jeb. Because he's too young to go to war, and Betsy's family is for the Union, and if they say anything bad about Jeb being a Rebel, it'll break my heart. Not that there's anything good to say about it. Plus, even if she doesn't bad-mouth Jeb, she'll feel sorry for me. I hate it when anyone feels sorry for me. I don't get to feel sorry for Betsy, because she doesn't have any brothers.

Let alone two brothers off fighting against each other.

4

During music period on Thursday, Amanda's class was learning Civil War songs for a Civil War concert that would be held in about a month. The music teacher, Mrs. Angelino, liked to tie the songs they sang to what they were learning in other subjects. She was old: she had been Amanda's father's music teacher when he had gone to Green Meadow Elementary thirty years ago and played the saxophone in the fifth-grade band.

Amanda wondered what Mrs. Angelino would think if she knew that little Tommy MacLeish was now all grown up and living at a Best Western motel because his wife didn't want him at home anymore.

Even though she was gray-haired and stout, Mrs. Angelino was full of energy. "All right, class!" she called out. "Everyone, watch me. Ricky, I think it's best if you and Lance aren't standing next to each other. Come over here by

Amanda. That's better. Now, here are the motions for 'Dixie Land.' "

Standing beside Amanda now, Ricky gave a loud groan.

"For 'I wish I was in the land of cotton,' you'll bend over like this and with your right hand pretend to be picking cotton. Bend over once on *wish* and a second time on *land*."

Mrs. Angelino did an emphatic cotton-picking demonstration while singing the opening line of "Dixie." She flashed the class a big, toothy smile as she sang, conveying the impression that cotton-picking was the most fun activity in the whole wide world. Amanda remembered Lance's diary: his slave boy hadn't thought it was pleasurable to pick cotton all day in the hot South Carolina sun. Out of the corner of her eye, she caught a glimpse of James watching Mrs. Angelino without expression.

" 'Old times there are not forgotten!' " Mrs. Angelino sang next. Her voice was high and quavery, like an opera singer's. For that line, she clasped her hands together over her heart, keeping the same blissful smile.

" 'Look away!' " She put one hand over her eyes and peered to the left.

" 'Look away!' " She jerked abruptly to peer toward the right.

" 'Look away!' " She peered straight ahead, gazing off expectantly into the distance.

" 'Dixie Land!' " She flung out both arms, as if she had finally spied Dixie Land after all her frenzied peering and was racing forward to embrace it at last.

"All right, class, now you try it." Vigorously, Mrs. Angelino began thumping out the music on the classroom's ancient upright piano.

Amanda picked her cotton, remembered old times, peered in all directions, and flung out her arms to welcome Dixie Land. Unfortunately, when Ricky flung out *his* arms to welcome Dixie Land, he whacked Amanda on the side of her head.

"Sorry," Ricky mumbled.

"Are you all right, Amanda?" Mrs. Angelino asked.

Amanda nodded, but she suddenly found herself blinking back scalding tears.

"Class, be careful when you fling out your arms. We don't want to be so excited about Dixie Land that we knock our classmates off the risers."

She went on showing the class motions for the rest of the song. For "I wish I was in Dixie! Hooray! Hooray!" they were to punch their fists into the air. "In Dixie Land I'll take my stand" was accompanied by an emphatic stomping of their feet. Most dramatic were the motions for the line "to live and die in Dixie." On "live" they stood up extra tall and straight, and then began crumpling into a wounded heap on "die," only to scramble back up in time to pound themselves on the chest on "Dixie." Were they singing in a bizarre new form of sign language for thoroughly confused deaf people?

Amanda noticed that some of the kids, like Patrick, weren't good at motions. Patrick tended to get his right hand or foot confused with his left. When everyone else took their stand in Dixie Land on their right foot, Patrick took his on his left. During concerts, Mrs. Angelino usually put Patrick in one of the back rows. Other kids, like Meghan, could have been professional actors, beaming out at the audience as they sang.

James, Amanda saw, did just enough gesturing to satisfy Mrs. Angelino. It would be a lot less risky standing next to him than to Ricky.

By now Ricky had changed the words of the song from "Dixie Land" to "Dixie cup." Amanda wondered if Dixie cups of ice cream had anything at all to do with the South. Maybe people ate more ice cream there because it was so much hotter than in the North.

"Oh, Dixie cup, I'll eat you up! I'd love to eat a Dixie!" Ricky sang. He tried out a spooning motion on the first line and a tummy-rubbing motion on the second.

"Ricky!" Mrs. Angelino called to him. "Watch me again. Like *this*." She repeated the correct motions, apparently unaware that Ricky was creating his own motions to be funny. Over the sound of the piano, she probably couldn't hear his new words. Amanda stifled a giggle. Every time Mrs. Angelino demonstrated the motions, she was as completely enthusiastic as she had been the first time. Amanda would have to ask her dad if Mrs. Angelino had stomped her feet and pounded her chest for Dixie thirty years ago, too.

The next time she saw him. At the Best Western pool.

★ ★ ★

After school, Amanda went with Beth to Beth's house. Beth's cat, Punkin, brushed up against Amanda's legs. Amanda reached down to stroke his soft fur. She and Steffi had both begged for a cat for years, but could never get one because their father was allergic.

"Hi, girls," Beth's mother greeted them. "Come have some apple-smoked Cheddar cheese that I got at the farmers' market. I got a half-bushel of Jonathan apples, too."

Amanda put some cheese and apple slices on her plate. All the plates at Beth's house were old, colorful, mismatched, bought for a dime or a quarter at a flea market or garage sale, usually with a story behind them.

"Where did this one come from?" Amanda asked. It was a nursery rhyme plate, with a picture of a chubby black-and-white cow jumping over a bright orange moon.

Beth's mother looked at it. "Oh, the cow! That was from a yard sale last spring. The woman was crazy about cows. Cow dish towels, cow salt-and-pepper shakers, cow teapots, cow place mats."

"If she loved cow things so much, why did she sell her cow plates?" Beth asked.

"She said that for Christmas and her birthday, her relatives sent her so many cow things that every few years she had to have a cow sale or her husband would divorce her."

Amanda stiffened. She hoped Beth and her mother didn't notice. That had to be the worst reason for a divorce that Amanda had ever heard.

Beth's plate was bright yellow, a plate full of sunshine. Amanda didn't ask its story.

The cheese was delicious, though more crumbly than store-bought cheese. The apple slices were firm and tart. Food always tasted so good at Beth's house. Beth's father appeared from his study and offered them some organic cider from the farmers' market, too.

Upstairs in Beth's room, Amanda pulled out her math homework. She liked to get math over with right away, and if there were any hard problems, Beth would help her. Beth was the best math student in the class, after James.

Amanda finished two problems—fractions—but then her thoughts wandered. If you took away one-fourth of a family, were three-fourths left? If you took away one-fourth of a family, Amanda wasn't sure you had a *family* left at all.

"Are you okay?" Beth asked. "You seem sad, or something."

Amanda couldn't bring herself to tell Beth, whose parents looked so contented as they handed out farmers' market snacks on whimsical storyland plates. Besides, maybe by suppertime, her father would have checked out of the motel and moved back home again. Every day, she still expected to walk in the door after school and find him there, unpacking his suitcase and admitting that the separation had been a terrible mistake.

"These problems are pretty hard."

"No, they're not! I'll help you. Let me run downstairs and get another apple and we can cut it up in pieces and do apple math. I'll bring some more cheese, too, and we can do cheese math."

Amanda forced a smile. "Okay."

While Beth was downstairs, Amanda gathered Punkin up onto her lap and tried to remember the last time her family had been happy together, like Beth's.

It wasn't last summer on their annual vacation to the beach. Steffi had said she didn't want to go at all if Tanya couldn't come with them, which had made Amanda feel that Steffi didn't care anymore about being sisters. Their mother had been seasick on the ferry ride over to Cape May and blamed their father because the excursion had been his idea in the first place. And then Steffi had gotten stung by a jellyfish and blamed everybody for making her go on the trip without Tanya.

Christmas? Amanda's parents had quarreled on Christmas morning, because her father had given her mother a nightgown she didn't like and was insulted he could even think she would like, and the whole argument took place in front of Grandpa and Grandma, visiting from Arizona, who had given both girls Barbies even though Steffi was in seventh grade then and Amanda had always hated Barbies.

But there had been one family night, a Friday night a few months ago, when Amanda's father decided to make fudge from scratch, using a candy thermometer they had gotten as a gift some other Christmas and never used. The fudge hadn't turned out—it was grainy instead of creamy, and refused to harden into a firm slab—but they had eaten all of it anyway, gobbling it from the pan with spoons, and her mother had laughed, and her father had kissed her mouth, which still had a smear of chocolate.

That had been a perfectly happy evening, the kind Beth's family had, except in Beth's family the fudge would have turned out if they had made it, but they wouldn't have made it because Beth's father didn't believe in eating processed sugar.

The next morning, though, Amanda's mother had seen the fudge-covered pots and pans all over the kitchen and had told her father that it was typical of him to make a big mess and leave it for someone else to clean up, and she was very sorry, but she wasn't his maid. Then she had left the house and slammed the door behind her.

Polly Mason might not know who was to blame in the Civil War, but Amanda knew it was the South; Polly would realize that someday. In the MacLeish family civil war, it was Amanda's mother who always spoiled things. Amanda didn't know why her mother couldn't see it, too.

"Apple math and cheese math!" Beth sang out, returning with two plates, a pink-flowered one holding apple slices and a daisy one holding cheese. Punkin jumped down from Amanda's lap and began meowing.

Amanda picked up her math homework. Unfortunately, Beth's well-meaning efforts couldn't do any good when the only math problem Amanda cared about was take away one father, and leave behind everybody else.

June 5, 1861

Dear Diary,

It is still too quiet at our house. There have been no battles yet. Everyone says the war will be over after the first battle, and the Union will win. I hope they are right, except that I wish the war could be over before the first battle. Then both of my brothers would come home again.

At school we are studying fractions. All of the answers on my slate are wrong. I am the worst dunce at fractions in the whole school. I feared that Master Taylor would make me sit on a stool in front of the class wearing a tall white dunce cap, but he did not. Maybe he knows that I am worried about my brothers. Of course, I was a dunce at fractions last year, too, before President Lincoln ever got elected and the South set itself against him.

After fractions, we sang songs. Our one-room schoolhouse has no piano, but Master Taylor plays the fiddle. We sang lots of different songs, and then Peter Partridge asked if we could sing "Dixie."

Master Taylor looked angrier than I have ever seen him. "I will not allow my pupils to sing a song in praise of any slave-holding states," he said. "I am loyal to my country, and I hope and expect that all of you are, too."

He told Peter Partridge to write one hundred times on the blackboard, "I will not sing 'Dixie.' " Peter Partridge told him that he would rather be whipped instead. Master Taylor said, "All right, young man, that can be arranged." He took the big stick he keeps by his desk and waved it at Peter. Peter said his father would whip Master Taylor if Master Taylor dared flog him for wanting to sing "Dixie." Then Peter took his slate and his lunch pail and walked out the front door and didn't return.

Master Taylor said we were done with music for today.

This was definitely the most exciting day our school has ever had. But I liked school better when it was less exciting.

I liked my family and my country better when they were less exciting, too.

5

Amanda's mother dropped Amanda and Steffi off in front of the Best Western office, next to the pool. "Room ninety-seven," she told them. "On the ground floor, around to the back. He'll give you a ride home."

The girls got out of the car. The September afternoon was hot enough for a swim, but they hadn't brought their suits. Amanda had thought of it—maybe it would make the visit feel more festive and fun—but decided against it. This wasn't a pool party, where she and Steffi would dunk each other during a lighthearted game of Marco Polo. Steffi had a grim, determined look on her face, as if she just wanted to get the whole thing over with.

"Seventy-two." Amanda read the number from one of the first doors they passed. Searching for their father's motel room, she felt a bit like a spy creeping through unfamiliar territory. Maybe she should make Polly Mason sneak away from home to spy for the North. Or for the South. She wasn't sure which side Polly would be spying for.

"It's this one," Steffi said, stopping before the door that said 97. "Go ahead and knock."

"No, you knock."

Steffi tossed back her hair. Then she rapped tentatively against the wooden door with her clenched knuckles.

Instantly the door swung open. "Girls! Come in!" Their father's tone was hearty, almost jovial. "You brought your suits, I hope. Go ahead and get changed. Last one to the pool's a rotten egg!"

"We didn't bring them," Steffi said coldly.

"I almost brought mine," Amanda added, so he'd know it was all right that he'd mentioned a swim. "But then . . . I guess I didn't."

Her father gave her shoulders a quick hug. "That's fine. Have a seat." He waved his hand expansively toward the inside of the room. "Sit anywhere."

The room had a large bed with a blue-patterned bedspread, a small sofa, and a stately-looking armchair with a low upholstered footstool in front of it. Amanda thought it was called a hassock—an old-fashioned-sounding word. Maybe Polly Mason's cabin could have a hassock in it. Though the Masons might not have any furniture that fancy.

Amanda looked at Steffi to see where Steffi was going to sit. When Steffi made no move to sit down, Amanda chose the armchair. Timidly she swung her feet up onto the hassock. It was comfortable. Polly Mason ought to have one.

Steffi continued standing long enough to make the moment stretch out awkwardly. Then she seated herself stiffly on the edge of the bed. Their father sprawled on the sofa, his long legs stretched out on the soft carpet.

No one spoke.

Amanda studied the picture hanging over the bed, a pleasant painting of a landscape with a small farmhouse next to a rolling field of golden hay. "That's a nice painting," she said.

"Which one?" her father asked.

Amanda pointed.

"Oh, that one."

The three of them looked at it, even Steffi. The farmhouse resembled Polly Mason's cabin. Amanda wondered if people grew hay in Maryland. She wondered if that *was* hay in the picture, or just some kind of golden grass. Or alfalfa, whatever alfalfa was. She tried to hear Mr. Mason's voice: "Jeb, Thomas, time to plant the hay!" "Jeb, Thomas, time to plant the alfalfa!" *Alfalfa* sounded better.

Steffi was the first to look away. She stared down at her nails. Amanda could see that the polish was half chewed off them. Steffi painted her nails so she'd stop chewing them, but then she chewed off the polish instead.

"Are you girls hungry? There are vending machines down the hall."

Steffi shook her head, so Amanda did, too. If only Steffi

weren't acting this way, it might have been fun to see what the machines had in them. Amanda enjoyed the kind of vending machines that had a little mechanical arm that reached up and grabbed each individual candy bar or bag of chips. It was like having an enchanted mechanical man at her service; her own private Tik-Tok of Oz.

"Or—wait! Let's go out for some ice cream. How does that sound? Banana splits? Hot fudge sundaes? We won't have to tell your mother."

It was the wrong thing to say. The joke might have worked in a happy family, but not when the parents weren't living together anymore.

"I'm not hungry," Steffi said.

"I'm not hungry, either," Amanda echoed.

"How's school?" their father tried. Amanda had known he would.

Steffi shrugged. Amanda wanted to tell him what was happening with her Civil War diary project, but she couldn't with Steffi there. Steffi would think it was babyish to be so enthusiastic about a dumb social studies assignment.

"We're still studying the Civil War," Amanda said. Somebody had to say something.

"Great! There's so much Civil War history right here in Maryland—Frederick, Antietam."

"We're going to have a class trip to Gettysburg."

"Great!" her father said again.

Steffi made a face. "We went there when I was in fifth

grade. The bus ride took forever, and one girl threw up, and then when we got there, it's this big field. We drove a whole hour each way to see a big field."

Amanda's father didn't reply, but he shot Amanda a sympathetic glance: a Civil War battlefield wasn't just any old big, boring field. Maybe next time Amanda could come to the Best Western alone and show her father what she had written so far in Polly Mason's diary.

Steffi clicked on the TV.

"Sure," their father said, "go ahead and see if any of your favorite programs are on."

Amanda didn't have any favorite programs; she didn't watch much TV. But Steffi was wild for cooking shows on the Food Network, even though, as far as Amanda knew, Steffi had never cooked anything in her life.

On the screen, there was a competition between teams of wedding cake bakers to build the most elaborate tiered wedding cake, covered with white-frosting leaves and vines and flowers and birds. Amanda began to get interested in spite of herself. "I hope Jennifer's team wins," she said.

"Pierre's team wins," Steffi said. "I've seen it before."

So much for any suspense. And Pierre's team did win, though Amanda still thought Jennifer's cake was prettier. She wondered what kind of wedding cake their parents had had. If she had seen a picture of it, she didn't remember what it looked like.

"We should go soon," Steffi said, looking at her watch

when the program was over. "I have a ton of homework for tomorrow."

And a ton of instant-messaging to do with Tanya, Amanda knew.

"Okay." Their father sounded almost relieved to have the visit over. From the top of the shiny, varnished bureau, he scooped up his car keys. "Bring your suits next time, and we can swim."

Steffi was already outside the door in the parking lot. Amanda turned toward her father and threw herself into his arms.

He held her close and patted her back. "It's okay, Mandy. It's going to be okay."

★ ★ ★

Amanda had hoped their father would come inside the house when he dropped them off, to say hello to their mother, check his mail, maybe even visit for a while longer. But he just pulled into the driveway and then pulled out again. He could have been someone else's father, giving them a ride home from a playdate.

"That was fast," their mother commented when they came into the kitchen.

"It's not that thrilling to sit around in a motel room," Steffi said.

Amanda wanted to defend their dad: they could have

brought their suits and gone for a swim; he had offered to buy them ice cream; he had tried to make conversation about school; he had acted interested in the Civil War. What more could he do?

For some reason, Steffi seemed to be siding with their mother, or at least siding against their dad. But he had to leave if his wife told him to go. Steffi was like Jeb, fighting for the South. Amanda was like Thomas, fighting for the North, for the side that deserved to win.

She longed to write another Polly Mason diary entry, but she always saved Polly for a reward after math homework, and this weekend the math homework was so hard that she had put it off as long as possible. At her desk, in her bedroom, she opened her math book and struggled for fifteen minutes with the least common denominator. It was a strange expression. You'd think you'd be trying to find the *most* common denominator, not the *least*. Not that it mattered. Amanda couldn't find any kind of common denominator at all.

Amanda's father was good at math, but it was too odd to call him at the Best Western Motel, especially after the strained visit just half an hour ago. Her mother could do Amanda's math problems fine herself, but she got impatient trying to explain them to Amanda. Things that were obvious to her seemed to need no explanation. "Just *think*, Amanda!" was one of her typically unhelpful remarks.

No one answered when Amanda called Beth's house.

Amanda remembered then that Beth was going on a long bike ride with her parents. Maybe because Beth was an only child, she and her parents did a lot of activities together.

Amanda had a thought. Before she could change her mind about it, she pulled out the school directory and called James.

His mother answered the phone. From the back-to-school open house, Amanda remembered that James's mother was white and his father was black. She almost hung up, but instead she made herself ask, "Is James there?"

"Just a minute, I'll get him. May I ask who's calling?"

It was too late to back out now. "It's Amanda. From school. I just have a question about the math homework."

A few moments later, James was on the line. "Hi, Amanda. What's up?"

"I was just wondering—the math homework? The least common denominator? Do you know how to find it?" *And why anyone would want to?*

"Sure." James acted as if girls called him all the time about math homework. Maybe they did.

After fifteen minutes, Amanda thought she understood the homework, though it would have been easier doing it together in person, instead of over the phone.

"Which Civil War person are you?" Amanda asked when they were finished. James hadn't volunteered yet for a turn to read any of his diary entries to the class.

"I'm Robert E. Lee."

"Wow!"

Mr. Abrams had assigned the characters randomly, he had said. Amanda felt luckier than ever to have gotten Polly, instead of Abraham Lincoln or Ulysses S. Grant. Though maybe if she had gotten Lincoln, he would have started to feel as real to her as Polly did now.

"What's happening so far to Robert E. Lee?" she asked.

"He just decided to fight for the Confederacy. He was really torn, you know. He opposed slavery—even freed his own slaves—and he loved the Union."

"So why did he fight for the South?"

"He loved Virginia more."

The simple, direct way James said it sent a little shiver down Amanda's spine. It made Lee's choice sound noble, and tragic.

"What about your girl?" James asked. "The one with the two brothers?"

"Polly. They left for the war, Jeb fighting for the South, Thomas fighting for the North. Now there's going to be the Battle of Bull Run."

"Do her brothers live through it? Or does one of them get killed?"

Amanda was flattered that James cared enough to ask. "I don't know. I haven't written it yet."

"I think they should live."

Amanda laughed. "I guess I should say that I hope Robert E. Lee wins the war, but I don't. And I know he doesn't."

An awkward pause followed. Amanda waited to see if James would say anything else, but he didn't.

"Anyway, thanks for the math help."

"Anytime."

Amanda hung up the phone, finished her awful math homework, and took out her Polly notebook. It was time for the first big battle of the Civil War to begin.

July 22, 1861

Dear Diary,

Oh, what a strange story I have to tell.

Mother and I were both feeling so sad and mopey, with the boys gone, that Father sent us to visit Aunt Sally and Uncle William in Washington. He stayed behind to take care of the farm. Mother and I took the stagecoach to Washington, and we're at Aunt Sally's fine house right now. I feel guilty that we left Father all alone. I hope he doesn't miss us too much.

Aunt Sally and Uncle William have no children, so they're not sure how to entertain a ten-year-old girl. Guess what they thought of. Yesterday they took us to see—a battle! The very first battle of this terrible war.

Lots of people went. Everyone knew it would be fought on the banks of a creek called Bull Run, because that's where the Union and Confederate troops were camping. So people came and brought picnics and sat on the grass overlooking the creek to watch it all, like a play in the theater, not that I've ever seen a play. Father thinks plays are sinful. If he doesn't want us watch-

ing plays, I wonder what he'd think about our watching a battle.

Aunt Sally brought a fine picnic for us—fried chicken and biscuits and butter and honey. She has a cook who is not a slave but a free black woman named Jessie Mae. Jessie Mae fried the chicken and churned the butter and made the biscuits.

From our grassy picnic place, we could see the blue of the Union troops and the gray of the Rebel troops. Gray seems a strange color for uniforms. Blue is so much brighter and braver-looking. Everyone said the blue uniforms would win the battle. The blue side would fire off a couple of cannons, with big scary booms, and shoot their rifles into the air, and the gray side would run away. And the war would be over.

I squinted as hard as I could into the distance, but I couldn't see any blue soldier who looked like Thomas, or any gray soldier who looked like Jeb. Probably the whole army didn't come for just one battle. Maybe my brothers were busy marching or setting up tents or fixing the fried chicken for the soldiers to eat for supper after the battle. Jeb fries chicken as well as Mother and I do, almost as well as Jessie Mae.

Then, oh, Diary, the battle began, and it wasn't at all like anyone expected. As long as I live, I'll never forget it. So many rifles firing, and smoke billowing everywhere, and the screams of dying soldiers, and wounded horses. The screams of the horses were the worst. And people running—the blue soldiers running, and the gray soldiers still firing, firing, firing. Constant firing and running and screaming. All the picnickers were running and screaming, too, leaving behind our tablecloths and chicken

55

and biscuits, hoping not to be trampled by the fleeing troops and the frightened horses. Mother and I ran as fast as we could, to the safety of Aunt Sally's wagon, but not fast enough to escape the sound of those screams.

And Mother and I didn't even know if Thomas and Jeb were there—Thomas firing, Jeb running—Jeb firing, Thomas running—both firing, both running.

Dear God, please let my brothers not have been at the Battle of Bull Run.

Please let them be sitting in their tents, Thomas in a tent for the North, Jeb in a tent for the South, safe and sound.

If they were there, then, if any soldiers fired at them, make it be that their bullets missed.

Please, dear God.

Amen.

6

"Who would like to share with us this morning?" Mr. Abrams asked on Friday as the class gathered on the floor by the rocking chair.

Even though she wanted to read her Battle of Bull Run diary, Amanda didn't raise her hand. It was her best entry yet. She had been thrilled when she read in one of their classroom Civil War books that people in the nation's capital had actually gone to watch the first battle of the Civil War as a picnic entertainment. That was the kind of strange and startling thing you couldn't just make up. But she didn't want to raise her hand to read every single day.

"Anyone we haven't heard from yet? Beth, how about you?"

Beth made a face, but opened her social studies notebook. "Mine is dumb," she warned.

"I doubt that very much," Mr. Abrams said.

"You haven't heard it yet."

"These are supposed to be real people's diaries, not great works of literature," Mr. Abrams reminded her.

Well, they could be both. Amanda wanted Polly's Civil War diary to be both.

"Okay. My person, Sarah Andrews, is the wife of a Civil War soldier who gets killed at the Battle of Bull Run. I don't want to write about the Battle of Bull Run till later, because then he'll be dead and my story will pretty much be over. So I'm trying to make time go by very slowly. So he won't be dead yet."

"That sounds like a good strategy," Mr. Abrams said.

" 'Thursday, June 6, 1861,' " Beth read. " 'Dear Diary. It is ten o'clock in the morning. It looks like it might rain. One drop just fell against the window. Then another drop fell. The log on the fire crackled. One piece of wood fell off the log. It made a loud sound. Now it is ten-oh-two.' "

Beth stopped reading. "The end."

Ricky and Lance laughed. Beth laughed, too. Even Mr. Abrams smiled.

"I told you it was dumb," Beth said good-naturedly.

Amanda raised her hand. "I don't think it's dumb. I like how she wrote down every tiny thing that happened in that one minute. That's what it's like when you're waiting, waiting, waiting for something to happen. She's waiting for her husband to come home. You'd expect time to move slowly, second by second by second."

"That's a good point," Mr. Abrams agreed. "Beth, what are you planning to have happen in your next entry?"

"It's going to stop raining. The sun is going to come out. Then it's going to go behind a cloud, and three more raindrops are going to fall."

The rest of the class laughed. It was hard not to. Beth was so clearly trying to make her diary entry sound as dull as possible, reciting each new line in a flat, expressionless, deadpan voice.

"But that *is* what it feels like to be all alone and waiting," Amanda tried again. "That's *exactly* what it feels like."

Suddenly she could see the young, lonely soon-to-be-widow so vividly in her mind's eye that she had to blink back tears. The minutes would seem even longer when she found out her husband was never coming back. Maybe for the rest of her life she'd count every raindrop as it fell.

"Who is willing to read next?" Mr. Abrams asked. "James?"

"Okay," James said, though Amanda knew that he wouldn't have volunteered to read if Mr. Abrams hadn't invited him.

James's entry was good, but long, written in a flowery, stilted style. James didn't usually write that way, so he must be trying to imagine how a well-educated southern gentleman would speak. He had obviously done a lot of research on the Second Battle of Bull Run. Amanda thought the diary entry would have been more interesting if he hadn't put in all the details about exposed left flanks and intercepted retreats. But maybe boys were interested in battles. Once again, Amanda was grateful that she had been assigned Polly, who could watch the battle from a safe, picnicking distance.

" 'And so, my esteemed diary,' " James read in conclusion, " 'today has been a day of great glory for our courageous men and their glorious cause. Long may the Confederacy endure!' "

Everyone clapped. Amanda wanted to jump right in to offer comments, but she had said so much about Beth's diary that she waited for someone else to take the first turn.

"It was *long*," Ricky said. "I mean, *long*. How did you write so much?"

James shrugged. What was he supposed to say?

"You did a lot of research," Meghan observed.

"Yes," Mr. Abrams said. "Your research was very impressive, James."

Amanda had waited long enough. "I loved the voice. It sounds just like I imagine Robert E. Lee sounding. Listening to it, you'd think James really supported the Confederacy, but you know he doesn't. Not in real life."

She hoped she wasn't jumping to conclusions about James just because he was black. Nobody supported the Confederacy nowadays. At least nobody Amanda knew.

"Many of you are doing a wonderful job of creating characters very different from yourselves," Mr. Abrams said. "We have time for one more. Any volunteers?"

Before Amanda could raise her hand, Lance beat her to it.

"Okay, Lance. Let's hear what your slave boy, Jonah, is doing these days."

Lance stood up to read. "The spelling is really bad, like before, but I'm just going to read it. You can imagine the bad spelling. Okay?"

Mr. Abrams nodded.

"It's, like, really bad spelling. Imagine the worst possible spelling, and that's what Jonah's spelling is like. 'Dear Diary.' This time I made it *d-i-r* for *dear*."

This was more excruciating than when Patrick read aloud and couldn't decipher his own handwriting. The way Lance kept pointing out how bad Jonah's spelling was, it was as if he was making fun of Jonah. Jonah couldn't help it if he couldn't spell. He had never been able to go to school the way Lance did. Who was Lance to be laughing at Jonah?

Amanda forced herself to stay calm. She reminded herself that Jonah was, after all, a completely fictitious character whom Lance himself had created. But still. She would never laugh at Polly. Authors shouldn't laugh at their characters in that sneering way, whatever their characters did or didn't do.

"Just keep on reading," Mr. Abrams suggested. It was amazing to Amanda that he could keep any sound of impatience from creeping into his voice.

" 'Dear Diary. My massah, he's off in the army. There be a big battle. Some place called Cow Run, I heerd.' See how he gets it all wrong? It's supposed to be Bull Run, but he calls it

61

Cow Run. 'I hope he gets hisself killed. His wife be just as bad. She kin whip us as hard as massah can. Too bad she not in the army, too.' The end."

Amanda wanted to tell Lance not to laugh at Jonah, but she didn't say anything. Probably the other kids suspected she thought her Polly diary was the best. She didn't want to sound conceited, picking faults in what the others had written.

Ricky said he liked everything about Lance's entry. And then it was time for math.

★ ★ ★

Saturday morning, Amanda lay in bed a long time. Usually she loved getting up early. Steffi and Beth were both night owls; Amanda didn't think Steffi would ever go to bed if their parents didn't make her. Well, if their mom didn't make her. Daddy wasn't there at bedtime anymore. Amanda was a morning person. She loved sitting at her desk writing, knowing that soon the first pink flush of dawn would be creeping over the low hills to the east.

This morning she didn't feel like getting up. It had been two weeks now since the Monopoly game; on Monday it would be two weeks since her father had left. Although he called every night at eight o'clock, Amanda had seen him only that one stiff, strained time at the motel. Last night, in his eight o'clock call, he had told her that he was moving today to an apartment. Having a father who lived in an apartment was less strange than having a father who lived in a motel. But it made the "separation" seem permanent, not temporary. People stayed in motels for a couple of days, maybe a couple of weeks. You could live in an apartment for a couple of months. Or a couple of years. Or the rest of your life.

Amanda looked at the clock by her bed. It was just past six-thirty. Steffi would sleep till noon. Even her mother would sleep late, till eight or nine; she didn't have to show any houses until after lunch. Nobody would know if Amanda slipped her bicycle quietly out of the garage and pedaled three miles to the Best Western Motel and back again.

In five minutes, she was dressed, her Civil War diary carefully protected by a plastic bag and tucked into her backpack in case it rained. She knew that rolling up the heavy garage door would make noise, so she walked her bike out of the side door in the garage that led to the path by her mother's flower beds. There was no rosy glow to the sky this morning, only a lightening of the gray clouds massed on the horizon. Amanda buckled on her bright yellow helmet and took off.

Hardly any cars passed her so early on a Saturday morning. An old man with a cane was walking a tiny dog; two women were jogging side by side; another woman was outside in her bathrobe picking up her newspaper. Houses gave way to shops, banks, a gas station. Then the road leading out of town started turning into more of a highway, and there was the Best Western. The water in the pool looked cold and forbidding. Only three cars were parked in the entire lot. One was her father's Toyota Camry, outside of Room 97.

It had been hard enough knocking at his door when Steffi had been with her and their father was expecting them. Amanda didn't have to be brave when Steffi was willing to be brave for both of them.

Amanda raised her hand to knock, but couldn't make herself go through with it.

She tried to pretend she was Steffi, drawing herself up taller, putting a bright, false, confident smile on her face. She still couldn't make her knuckles rap against the door.

It was easier to pretend she was Polly. All she did these days, practically, was pretend she was Polly. But Polly was hardly braver than Amanda. Polly hadn't had to do anything brave yet. At the picnic by Bull Run, Polly had panicked like everyone else.

Maybe Amanda wouldn't have to knock. Maybe her father would come out to the car with his suitcase, so he could drive to the new apartment bright and early and start getting settled in.

Maybe he'd sense her presence outside his room. "Mandy!" he'd say joyfully as he flung open the door. "I had a feeling I'd find you here!"

Another minute went by.

Just knock!

Amanda did it, one timid little knock, then another. No

one answered. Maybe her father was in the shower. Or still asleep. She knocked more loudly.

Did she hear footsteps?

Then the door opened, just a crack, and her father peered out at her from behind the short length of heavy chain that kept the door from opening farther. He was wearing his pajama bottoms. His hair stood up every which way. "Amanda! What happened? What's wrong?"

Plainly she had startled him.

"Nothing. I just came to visit." That didn't seem reason enough to show up unannounced so early in the morning. "I—I brought my Civil War diary for you to see. You know, the social studies project I've been telling you about."

"Does your mother know you're here?"

He still hadn't opened the door. The chain between them made her feel that she was visiting him in prison, talking to him through a grille of iron bars.

"No. She was sleeping."

"Mandy." She could see the strain in his face. "Your mother is going to be worried when she wakes up and finds you gone. It's not a good time, honey. I'm moving today—I told you—and your mother will be furious with me if you worry her like this."

Amanda tried to say that it was all right. She should have known all along that it was a bad idea to visit, a bad, dumb, *stupid* idea. But no words would come.

"Mandy, honey, go wait by the car while I throw on some

clothes. We can toss your bike in the trunk, and I'll give you a ride home. I won't be a minute."

"Okay." Amanda forced the word out.

The door shut, with her father on one side of it and Amanda on the other.

He had never even taken off the chain.

Suddenly all of Amanda's timid hesitation turned to fury. He should have wanted her to be there. He should have welcomed her into his room with a warm, grateful hug. What kind of father turned his own daughter away from his door?

Trembling with anger, Amanda jumped on her bike and started pedaling. She didn't need for him to drive her home; she didn't need to show him her Polly diary; she didn't need for him to open the motel room door and be a real father; she didn't need him at all for anything, ever.

She was almost glad when it started to rain. Somehow it seemed to serve him right that she was cold and miserable. At least Polly's diary was safe and dry in its plastic bag inside her backpack.

A few blocks later, a car slowed beside her. Afraid to let herself hope it was her father, Amanda pedaled faster.

"Mandy!" she heard her father call through the open car window. "Honey, please, let me drive you home. I don't want you riding by yourself in the rain."

Amanda halted by the side of the road. More than anything, she longed to give in, to let her father's strong hands relieve her of her dripping bike, to slip into the front seat of the car beside him and warm herself by his car heater, while she cried on his broad shoulder.

But she couldn't forget that chain on his door.

"I'm fine!" she spat at him. "I'm practically home now. And I'm not a baby!"

"Mandy . . ." He sounded almost pleading.

Without another word, Amanda started riding again, refusing to turn to look at him as he slowly drove behind her the rest of the way home.

Her mother and sister were still sleeping when Amanda crept into the house. After changing back into her pajamas, she hung her damp clothes over the shower rod. Then she climbed into bed, shivering, and let herself be Polly for a while.

July 27, 1861

Dear Diary,

It has been six days since the Battle of Bull Run. We still have not heard anything about Jeb and Thomas. Surely if they were injured—or worse—someone would have gotten word to us. But maybe not. There was so much chaos and commotion that day. Those caring for the wounded and burying the dead might be too busy to take pen and paper to write to the families of the fallen men.

Mother and I are back on the farm. We are glad to be here.

The waiting would be even harder if we were away from home, and from Father. If any bad news comes to us, we will be able to bear it better together.

This afternoon the newspaper will arrive from Washington. Father thinks they will have a list of the dead and wounded. I am going to walk into town to pick up a copy at Mr. Scott's store.

It seems that the morning will never pass. Blackie is restless, too. She climbed up onto my lap and settled down as if to purr. Then she saw a fly and leaped out of my lap again. It is starting to rain. One raindrop slides down the window. Then another.

★ ★ ★

The rain stopped and I walked to town. Mr. Scott had the papers. He handed mine to me. I ran far away from the crowd in front of the store so I could look at the list of names alone. They were printed on the front page. No news in the world was more important than whether or not my brothers were still alive.

I could not make myself look. The longer I went without looking, the longer it seemed that both of them might be alive.

But Mother and Father were waiting.

I had to be brave, as brave as my brothers.

I stared down at the paper. There were two lists: Union dead and wounded, Confederate dead and wounded. I scanned the Union list first and found the M's. Mason, Robert—dead. Matthews, Donald—wounded. No Mason, Thomas. I checked the list again to be sure. Thomas's name was not there.

Then I looked at the Confederate list. I saw it right away:
Mason, Jebediah—wounded.

Jebediah.

Jeb.

Wounded.

Not dead, but wounded.

My brave, kind, funny, caring, favorite brother: wounded.

7

Amanda hadn't known herself what Polly would see when she searched for her brothers' names in the newspaper listings. Maybe she should have made Thomas wounded instead of Jeb? No, it had to be Jeb. Sometimes when you wrote something, you knew that the story you were making up was the story that had to be.

Downstairs in the kitchen, Amanda's mother was emptying the dishwasher. Amanda could hear the brisk clink of one plate against another. She wondered if her father had called: the phone had rung twice, but the caller had hung up before the answering machine clicked on. Amanda had a feeling her father didn't want her mother to hear his message and know what had happened.

Amanda heard Steffi's door open. She hopped out of bed and hurried to the hall. "Steffi?"

Her sister's hair was tangled from sleep, and her eyes were still half shut. "Yeah?"

Amanda plunged ahead. "Can we talk?"

Steffi scowled. Their father used to tease Steffi about waking up on the wrong side of the bed, until he realized that calling attention to Steffi's morning crabbiness only made her even crabbier.

"It's important."

Steffi rubbed her left eye. "Does it have to be now?"

"I went to see Dad."

Instantly, Steffi was awake. "Does Mom know?"

Amanda shook her head. "I went on my bike, while you guys were sleeping."

"And?"

"It was awful." The swollen lump stuck in Amanda's throat. "It was like—I could tell he didn't want me to be there."

"How early was it?"

"It was early—like seven? But—Steffi—he didn't even open the door all the way. There was this chain thing on it. You know, so burglars can't come in? And he didn't take it off. Like I was a burglar."

Amanda's voice was shaking so much she couldn't keep on speaking.

Without a word, Steffi led the way into Amanda's room and lay down on the bed, patting the spot next to her. Amanda followed. Steffi pulled up Amanda's bright patterned quilt so that it covered both of them. For a while both girls were silent.

"Do you think someone else was there?" Steffi finally asked.

At first Amanda didn't understand the question. "I told you, it was early. It was barely even light yet. Who has company at seven in the morning?"

"Amanda," Steffi said, gently but knowingly.

Suddenly Amanda realized what Steffi meant.

"No!" Their dad wasn't a movie star on location, meeting another lady movie star. "That couldn't be! We would have known. Mom would have known."

"Maybe Mom *does* know."

How could Steffi say such a terrible thing in such a calm, quiet voice? But Amanda could feel that beside her in the bed, Steffi was trembling.

"We could ask Mom," Amanda suggested tentatively.

"No!" Steffi sounded almost angry now. "Don't you dare ask her. What if she doesn't know? Maybe it's a one-time thing, and it'll be over before Mom ever finds out. I don't think she *does* know. This is something new. I know it is."

"So what should we do?"

"We have to find out ourselves."

"Like how?"

"We look for clues." Steffi sat up in the bed and clasped her hands around her bent knees. "Go get a notebook. A small, secret notebook."

If there was one thing Amanda had an abundance of, it was notebooks. She was always buying them in different

72

sizes, colors, wide-ruled paper, college-ruled paper, spiral-bound, marble-covered. From her stash in the drawer in the nightstand next to her bed, she selected the smallest one, with a dark blue cover.

"Okay," Steffi said. "Don't write anything on the first page, in case Mom or someone else opens it. Start on page three. Write 'Possible Clues.' "

Amanda obeyed. She was grateful when Steffi was like this, bold, confident, in the grip of a plan, willing to include Amanda instead of leaving her out.

"Number one," Steffi dictated. "Lipstick on his collar."

"What?"

"Just write it down. That's almost always the first clue: a bright red lipstick smear on the man's shirt collar."

Once again, Amanda was amazed by the things Steffi knew, things she was sure they didn't teach in middle school.

"Number two. A long blond hair on his jacket. Well, any hair that doesn't look like his, or Mom's."

Amanda hadn't even written down number one yet. "Should I be writing these in code?" Amanda asked.

Steffi considered the question. "Maybe. Write *LOC* for Lipstick on Collar. And *LBH* for Long Blond Hair. Then write *CCB*."

"What's *CCB*?"

"Credit Card Bills. You know, for flowers, or candy, or fancy restaurants."

"Anything else?"

"*CPC*. Cell Phone Charges. That's probably the biggest one. If we can find out if he's started calling some woman all the time on his cell phone, then we'll know."

Amanda stared at the list: *LOC*, *LBH*, *CCB*, *CPC*.

"I'm not sure I want to know," she whispered.

"I'm not sure I do, either," Steffi admitted. "But we already do know, don't we? Once he didn't take that chain off the door, we knew."

★ ★ ★

That afternoon, Amanda went with Beth's parents to see a matinee performance by Beth's Irish dancing school. Amanda's mother didn't come with them; despite Amanda's friendship with Beth, the two families weren't close. Amanda's parents always made jokes about how much granola Beth's parents ate, even though Amanda had never seen anyone eating granola at Beth's house. She knew the joke meant they thought Beth's parents were hippies, left over from the 1960s.

Beth was already at the Arts Center, so Amanda sat alone in the backseat while Beth's mother drove, and Beth's father sat next to her, complaining.

"Look at all these cars. We should have bicycled," he commented as they waited at the first traffic signal. The red light glistened on the dark pavement.

"In the pouring rain?"

"We have rain gear. Lots of people cycle in the rain. In Copenhagen, everyone bikes everywhere in all kinds of weather."

"This isn't Copenhagen."

Amanda giggled. For some reason, Beth's parents' conversations always struck her as funny, whereas if her own parents had said the very same things, the conversation would have felt tense, strained, even hostile. If her mother had said, "This isn't Copenhagen," it would have come out as, "If you think Copenhagen is such a cycling paradise, why don't you go live there?" When Beth's mother said it, it came out as, "You are an impractical dreamer, and that's why I love you."

The light changed, and Beth's mother drove on. "I hope Beth's number goes well," she said. "She seemed so nervous about it last night."

"She wasn't really," Amanda offered. "Sometimes Beth says she's nervous, but she doesn't mean it. It's just a thing you say before a concert. Beth never worries."

"Everyone worries," Beth's mother said.

Well, certainly Beth didn't worry the way that she, Amanda, worried.

"If all the bicycles in the rest of the world become cars, everyone will have plenty to worry about," Beth's father said. "We haven't even seen the start of global warming yet. Wait till those billions of cars start emitting their greenhouse gases."

"Okay, we should have bicycled," Beth's mother said.

Amanda didn't feel like giggling this time. It hadn't been one bit of fun biking home from the motel eight hours ago, tears mixing with raindrops on her wet face.

The recital was excellent. Amanda loved to watch Irish dancers, their feet clattering and stomping so furiously that her own feet started to twitch in rhythm. To Amanda's surprise, James and his parents were in the audience. There was a black girl in the beginning class; she must have been James's younger sister. Maybe Amanda shouldn't have been surprised: not every black person had to do African dancing.

Beth and Meghan were in the advanced class. In Amanda's opinion, Beth was the best, though Meghan was an excellent dancer, too. Both girls' feet never faltered, and their smiles never faded, even though it had to be exhausting to dance like that. Amanda clapped until her palms stung.

The fiddle music sang inside her as she filed out of the auditorium behind Beth's parents to the reception set up in the lobby. Polly would have danced to that kind of old-time music. Except that Polly was hardly in the mood for dancing these days, with Jeb lying wounded somewhere.

While Amanda waited for Beth to appear, she walked across the lobby to say hello to James.

"Hi," she said.

"Hi," he said.

"Was that your sister?" As soon as she said it, she knew it was a stupid question. There was only one black dancer in the whole concert, and James and his father were the only black people in the audience.

"Uh-huh," he said.

"How did she get interested in Irish dancing?" That was a legitimate question you could ask anybody.

"She saw an Irish dancing show on TV. But she likes all kinds of dancing—she's taken classes in tap dancing, too."

Amanda thought of James standing so stiff on the risers during "Dixie," hardly doing the song motions at all.

"But you don't like dancing. I mean, do you?" Had she asked another dumb question?

Luckily, James laughed. "How did you guess?"

Relieved, Amanda laughed, too. Then James drifted away to look for his sister, and Amanda rejoined Beth's parents at the refreshment table. A few minutes later, Beth greeted them there, her cheeks aflame from dancing.

Amanda hugged her. "You were wonderful!"

Then her parents hugged her. "Wonderful!" they echoed.

Beth flashed the same big smile she had worn throughout her dance. "I was pretty good," she conceded. "Okay, I was wonderful."

"I never understand how you can remember all the steps," Amanda said.

"You don't have to remember them. You hear the music, and your feet just start doing them." Beth gulped down her punch. "I'm hot. Are the rest of you hot?"

"The rest of us haven't been dancing Irish jigs," her father said.

"Let's go outside," Beth told Amanda. To Amanda's relief, Meghan, busy with her own family, didn't join them.

Together the two girls stood under the awning over the Arts Center entrance. The rain pounded the blacktop, like millions of tiny dancing feet. Amanda liked that simile. She hadn't been using enough similes in Polly's journal.

"What did you guys do this morning?" Beth asked.

Amanda swallowed hard before she replied. She couldn't hide the truth from Beth forever. "Well, things have been sort of strange at my house."

"Strange how?"

I went to visit my dad at his motel, and he wouldn't let me in.

"Well, you know how my parents fight a lot?"

Beth looked uncomfortable. "They don't fight that much. At least when I'm there. And my parents fight, too. Sometimes my mother secretly dries the laundry in the clothes dryer when my father isn't home so he won't see that she didn't hang it up on the clothesline."

Amanda's parents had always quarreled about trivial things. But in their case the triviality of the cause made the fight itself seem more, not less, serious.

"So did they have a fight today?" Beth asked.

"I guess you could call it that." A very long fight that had been going on and on for weeks without any yelling, or even any speaking. The gap between Amanda's world and

Beth's world was too huge to bridge in one quick conversation.

Beth shrugged. "Don't let it get you down."

The advice was so breezy and unhelpful that Amanda's stomach tightened.

When Amanda didn't say anything in reply, Beth changed the subject. "Did you write more Polly?"

Amanda nodded.

"I'm getting where I can't stand Sarah Andrews. I'm starting to hate her. I think I'm going to kill off her husband in the next entry and just get it over with. She needs to get on with her life. She can't sit around forever counting raindrops."

"Maybe you need a subplot. You know, something else that can happen to her."

"Like what?"

"I have to think." Amanda didn't know Sarah as well as she knew Polly.

"Can I come over and we can think together? My mom's canning tomatoes, and our house stinks. It's like living in a catsup factory."

Amanda didn't know what to say. That would be one way for Beth to find out that Amanda's father didn't live there anymore. But it wasn't fair that Beth's mother was canning tomatoes and her father was grumbling about global warming, while Amanda's family lay in pieces, like a shattered jar of tomatoes.

"So can I?" Beth asked again.

"It's . . . not a good time," Amanda said. With a start, she realized that it was the same line her father had used that morning at the motel.

Cars were starting to leave the parking lot. In the glare of the sweeping headlights, Beth looked surprised, then hurt. She waited, as if expecting Amanda to explain.

Meghan appeared in the doorway of the Arts Center and waved to them, or maybe just to Beth. "Beth!" she called. "My parents want to say hi to you."

Without another word, the two girls went back inside. The tray of cookies was almost empty now, with only a few broken bits and crumbs left behind. Someone had spilled punch on the white tablecloth, leaving a damp pink stain. If Amanda's mother had been there, Amanda knew she would have said that a stain like that one would never come out, no matter how hard you scrubbed at it. A stain like that would last forever.

July 29, 1861

Dear Diary,

Wounded *could mean anything. It could mean that a bullet struck Jeb's shoulder. It could mean that he broke his leg. Hurt shoulders and broken legs heal. But what if they had to cut off Jeb's arm or leg? What if Jeb never gets well again?*

Father and Mother are trying to find out more. Father sent a telegram to the army office in Washington. Every hour I look down the road to see if a telegram is coming to us in reply.

I want to know the truth. And I don't want to know the truth. But I want to know more than I don't want to know.

I think.

Fear is pounding inside my head like a million tiny marching feet.

My family was already broken, once Jeb and Thomas left us to fight on opposite sides in this terrible war. But now, with Jeb wounded, we feel like a shattered jar of Mother's best tomatoes, spreading out in a bloody-looking mess on her clean kitchen floor.

"Where is he?" I asked Father.

Father said he didn't know. There is a military hospital in Washington, near Aunt Sally's house. Aunt Sally went there to check for us. But her letter came this morning saying that she didn't find Jeb in Washington. Father said there are troops farther south, in Virginia. I think Father or Mother should go look for him there. Father said he has to stay home to do the farming, and an army camp is no place for a woman.

I have an idea, dear Diary.

An army camp may be no place for a woman, but it might be a place for a girl. For a girl dressed as a boy.

The million marching feet in my head are a million dancing feet now. I can tuck up my hair under one of Jeb's old caps. I can wear his oldest, smallest shirt and trousers. I can find my brother and nurse him back to health and bring him safely home.

★ ★ ★

In the morning I rose very early, while even Father was still sleeping. I put on Jeb's clothes and wrapped some bread and cheese and apples in my old shawl. I hugged Whitie and Blackie. I wrote a note for Father and Mother and left it under the pillow on my bed so that they would find it, but not too soon.

Gone to find Jeb.
Love, Polly

8

"*Go ahead, girls, and get your raincoats on,*" Amanda's mother said on Sunday afternoon.

Steffi glanced at her watch. "It's only two-twenty, and Dad's not going to be here until two-thirty."

"He might come early."

He never arrived anywhere early, but Amanda didn't feel like arguing. From the hall closet, she retrieved her green rain slicker and Steffi's purple one. She didn't want her father to come to the door and ring the bell and have her mother open it.

"All it does anymore is rain," Steffi grumbled as she grabbed her raincoat from Amanda, but didn't put it on.

"Speaking of rain, why were your damp clothes hanging in the bathroom yesterday, Amanda?"

Amanda shot Steffi a look of mute appeal. How could she have been so careless as to leave her wet things there for her mother to find?

"She got soaked when she went out to get the mail." Steffi lied so deftly that Amanda almost found herself believing it was true.

"We only have ten umbrellas in the house. Why doesn't anybody ever use one? Amanda, run and get one for each of you."

Steffi still hadn't put on her rain slicker. "We're not going that far, just from the house to the car and from the car to Dad's apartment."

Amanda fetched the umbrellas. It felt far to her. It felt like going on a voyage to the dark side of the moon.

"You'll have to tell me all about it!" their mother said brightly.

"An apartment is just an apartment," Steffi said.

"Fine. Don't tell me, then."

"All I said was that an apartment is an apartment. I mean, that's true. An apartment *is* an apartment. That's all I said."

"That's not all you meant."

"He's here!" Amanda interrupted gratefully. "Bye!" she called back over her shoulder, and then wished she hadn't turned around to see her mother's face crumpling into tears.

Without bothering to put up her umbrella, she fled out the door to her father's waiting car. Steffi pounded right behind her, shrugging on her raincoat as she went.

Steffi slipped into the front seat next to their dad; Amanda took the backseat.

"Are you ready to honor my humble abode with your illustrious presence?" their dad asked. The fancy words were obviously intended to be funny, but Amanda didn't think it was funny that he had a new abode, instead of the same old familiar abode with his wife and daughters.

Seated directly behind him, she had a good view of his dark green jacket. No long blond hairs, or hairs of any kind, were visible. His shirt collar was hidden by his coat, but she couldn't believe there was lipstick on it. Amanda didn't know any women who wore lipstick. Their mother didn't. Mrs. Angelino didn't.

For the first time, it occurred to Amanda that Steffi might be wrong: about long blond hairs, bright red lipstick, lady movie stars, everything.

Loud rap music blared from the car radio: Steffi's choice. Their mother would have made Steffi turn it off, but their father started tapping his hand on the steering wheel in time to the beat. Amanda's heart hurt to see him trying so hard, even though she still hadn't forgiven him for leaving the chain on the door at the motel. She had made sure to be in the bathtub washing her hair when he called last night.

"Don't," Steffi snapped at him. The tapping stopped.

The car turned into the parking lot of an apartment complex called Georgetown Meadows. All the buildings were two-story red brick, with little brick pathways leading up to them, like Colonial Williamsburg. Maybe like the Civil War, too. Probably concrete or cement or asphalt hadn't been invented during the 1860s.

Amanda wondered if telegrams had been invented then. She'd have to look that up when she got home. The diary would feel fake if Polly's family was sending telegrams thirty years before telegrams existed. Were telegrams sent by electricity? Had electricity been discovered yet? Actually, now that Amanda considered the question, it would be better if they couldn't send a telegram. That would give Polly more of a reason to set out to find Jeb herself.

Leaving their umbrellas behind in the car, Amanda and Steffi ran with their father to his apartment door. Outside, the apartment looked old, but inside, it looked new, with freshly painted white walls and spotless, light wall-to-wall carpet. Amanda had never seen the furniture before; her dad hadn't taken any of it from home.

"The apartment came furnished," he explained, although neither girl had asked. "I figured furniture is furniture."

An apartment is an apartment.

He hung up their raincoats in the front closet, empty except for a few wire hangers. They all sat down in the living room, Amanda and Steffi side by side on the flowered couch, their father facing them in a wingback chair.

Amanda wondered if he would ask them about school or offer to take them out for ice cream.

"Do you want a tour of the rest of it?" he asked.

Steffi shook her head. Amanda shook hers, too.

"TV?" He tossed Steffi the remote. "I have cable."

Steffi clicked it on. It was a relief to hear the sounds of other people's lives.

"Mandy?" he said then. "About yesterday morning."

Amanda saw Steffi stiffen, even as she kept on flipping through the channels.

"I understand," Amanda said quickly. "It was too early. You didn't know I was coming."

"No," he said. "The night before, I had dinner at the crab house at the mall, and there was something off about the crabs. Either that, or I was coming down with a twenty-four-hour stomach flu. I was sick as a dog all night and still getting up to be sick until checkout time at eleven. I can't remember when I've felt worse."

He *had* looked terrible at the motel, that ghastly greenish pale of being about to throw up. And even so, he had been willing to get in the car and drive her home.

The huge crushing rock of sadness lifted from Amanda's chest as if a kindly giant had reached down and gathered it up, saying, "You don't need to carry this. It's too heavy for you." The instant she got home, she was going to tear out the notebook page of Possible Clues and burn it. Or chew it up and swallow it, like the stupid spy she was done pretending to be.

She tried to catch Steffi's eye, but Steffi had found her very favorite cooking show on the Food Network and was staring straight ahead at the TV screen.

"Do you feel okay now?" Amanda asked.

"You bet. But no more crab sandwiches for me for a while."

Amanda had never liked crab sandwiches, with the crab's legs hanging out over the ends of the bun. She felt sick herself just thinking of them.

"Wasn't there something you wanted to show me?" he asked.

"Just that school thing I was telling you about, the Civil War diary."

"Do you have it with you now?"

"No." She wouldn't have shown it to him in front of Steffi. And she wouldn't have shown it to him if she thought he was seeing some lady.

"Bring it next time. I'm so proud of your writing, Mandy. You really have a knack for putting words together. I still have every Father's Day poem you ever wrote for me, you know."

Amanda waited for Steffi to make her usual retching, gagging sound: Steffi always teased her about writing sappy poems for family members on special occasions. But Steffi didn't seem to be listening to their conversation. Whatever thirty-minute meal was being prepared on the cooking show was apparently absorbing all her interest.

"Okay!" their dad announced heartily. "We're not going to spend this whole visit watching TV. I'm going to be away next weekend on a business trip. So today we're going to have a father-daughter outing."

Amanda stood up. Steffi stayed seated.

"Come on, Steffi, honey, you can catch the show later."

"What kind of outing?" Steffi sounded so hostile, even for Steffi, that Amanda was taken aback. Had Steffi really tuned out the whole conversation about the crab sandwiches?

"Too bad you didn't bring umbrellas. We could take a walk in the rain. I remember when you girls thought it was the most fun thing in the whole world to put up your little Barney umbrellas and go out stomping in every puddle."

"We did bring umbrellas. They're in the car," Amanda said.

His face lit up. "Great!"

"Things have changed, Dad," Steffi said coldly. "For your information, we're not five years old anymore. We don't have Barney umbrellas. We don't stomp in puddles."

His smile faded. "I'm aware of that, Steffi. I know things have changed. Believe me, I know."

"Should I go get the umbrellas?" Amanda asked.

"No," Steffi said.

"I guess not," her dad said in a low, defeated tone.

Amanda couldn't bear it. She wasn't going to let Steffi ruin everything. "I want to walk in the rain."

This time Steffi included Amanda in her glare. Amanda's chin lifted.

Their dad looked from one daughter to the other. "Okay," he finally said. "Steffi, you can stay here and finish watching your show. Amanda and I won't be gone long."

It was raining harder now than when they had arrived. Amanda didn't care. Her shoes were soaked by the time they reached the tennis courts at the edge of Georgetown Meadows, but the red and yellow leaves starting to turn on the overhanging oak and maple trees shone in the soft lamplight. No, not *red* and *yellow—scarlet* and *golden.*

"Daddy?"

"Yes, Mandy?"

"Do you know when telegrams were invented?"

He chuckled, obviously having expected a different kind of question. "They've been around for a long time. I think they date back to the early 1800s."

"So they were around during the Civil War?"

"I'm sure they were."

That was okay. Amanda wouldn't have to go back and change her last diary entry, the one with the telegram in it. And Polly could still have a reason to go looking for Jeb, even if telegrams had been invented. There could be lots of reasons why a telegram about Jeb wouldn't have come to the Mason family. Maybe Jeb had amnesia and couldn't remember his name. Maybe there was no telegram-sending machine at a makeshift army hospital during wartime.

They kept on walking. Autumn was her favorite time of year, Amanda decided. And walking in the rain with her father, on a gray and gloomy, sodden and sopping October afternoon had just become Amanda's favorite thing in the world to do.

Dear Diary,

The sky was growing pink when I reached the village, but no one was awake to see me slip down Main Street past the general store. I kept on walking south, toward Washington. That was the only idea I had so far.

The next village was four miles away. I stopped there to pump myself some water from the village well and eat my breakfast. A lady at the well said, "Good morning, young man," and at first I didn't know she was talking to me! Then I jumped up to curtsy and remembered in time to bow instead. I couldn't take off my hat because it hid my hair. I'm sure the lady thought me very rude.

What if she had asked my name and I had said Polly Mason? I hadn't thought of what my new name should be. Since Paul sounds a bit like Polly, I decided to be Paul Mason.

By the next town, my feet were tired. I like to walk, but not for hour after hour in the hot July sun. I had to sit and rest under a tree. I wondered if Mother and Father had found my note yet. Maybe Father would come after me in the wagon. I half wanted him to come so I wouldn't have to walk anymore. But if he came, I wouldn't find Jeb.

I started walking again. A farmer's wagon pulled up, not Father's. "Do you want a ride, young man?" the farmer asked.

"Yes, sir," I told him, trying to make my voice deeper. "I'm going to Washington."

"Why are you going there?" he asked.

I couldn't think of a good lie. Jeb was always better at lying than I was. "I'm going to find my brother. He's been wounded in the war."

"Where is he?" the farmer asked.

"I don't know," I said.

Then, Diary—oh, I am ashamed to write this—I started to cry. Imagine Paul Mason there by the side of the road crying! With no handkerchief, either!

"Now, now, laddie," the man said. "I'll take you to the army hospital in Washington."

"My aunt already went there and she couldn't find him."

"Is your brother Union or Rebel?" the man asked.

I told him Rebel.

Then the man looked angry, like Master Taylor about to whip Peter Partridge for wanting to sing "Dixie."

"Are you a Rebel, too, lad?" he asked me in a harsh voice.

I shook my head. "I don't know what I am. My brother Thomas is for the North, and my brother Jeb is for the South, but I'm not for either side. I just want to find my brother."

Then the man smiled.

"There's a Rebel hospital in Virginia," he said. "I will take you there."

I climbed into his wagon, in the back, on top of his hay. Or maybe it is alfalfa. I am sitting there now, dear Diary, writing to you.

I don't know where Jeb is, but I have to believe I'm going to find him.

Sometimes you just have to believe.

9

On Thursday, Mrs. Angelino told Amanda's class that they were going to be learning a new Civil War song called "Goober Peas."

"Does anyone know what goober peas are?" she asked.

Amanda didn't. She wondered if Polly did.

Without raising his hand, Ricky called out, "Boogers?" He and Lance started laughing so hard they almost fell off the music room risers.

"No," Mrs. Angelino said pleasantly, as if Ricky had offered a sensible, but unfortunately mistaken, answer. "Lance, why don't you come stand over here by me."

Every class Lance and Ricky started out standing next to each other, and every class Mrs. Angelino decided that they needed to be separated. At least this time Amanda was safe, sandwiched between Beth and Meghan.

"Goober peas are peanuts," Mrs. Angelino explained, apparently deciding against asking for any more guesses from the class. "Peanuts were a popular crop in the South, and the Confederate soldiers liked to eat them as a healthy snack. The great African American scientist George Washington Carver found three hundred different uses for peanuts. Isn't that amazing?"

She beamed at James, as if George Washington Carver had been his great-grandfather.

"How many uses for peanuts can you think of, boys and girls?"

"Putting them up your nose!" Ricky suggested.

Everybody laughed, except for Mrs. Angelino. "Peanut oil is one," she said. "And of course peanut butter. So every time you eat a peanut butter and jelly sandwich, you have a wonderful African American scientist to thank." She smiled at James again.

"But all that happened long after the Civil War. During the Civil War, what the soldiers did with peanuts, or goober peas, was eat them. And that's what we're going to be singing about now."

Mrs. Angelino pointed to the words of the song, written up on the chalkboard. "Sitting by the roadside, on a summer's day. Chatting with my messmates, passing time away. Lying in the shadows, underneath the trees. Goodness, how delicious, eating goober peas."

Amanda thought of Polly, stretched out on the fresh alfalfa, or hay, in the back of the farmer's wagon. "Goober

Peas" was good music for a long lazy day with nothing to do.

Amanda's class had plenty to do, however. Mrs. Angelino proceeded to show them the motions for each line. For "Sitting by the roadside," they plunked their arms down as if seating themselves in a chair. For "Chatting with my messmates," they turned to the person next to them and moved their hands like talking puppets. For "Lying in the shadows," they placed both hands, like a pillow, on the right side of their heads. For the last line they pantomimed putting peanuts into their mouths.

Or, in Ricky's case, into his nose. Amanda could hear that he was singing "booger peas" instead of "goober peas." She smothered a giggle.

After three times through the song, Mrs. Angelino was flushed from her enthusiastic pretend-devouring of goober peas. Signaling to the class to sit down on the risers, she lowered herself heavily into her chair.

"For our concert," Mrs. Angelino said, "I want to add some variety to the program. So in addition to our Civil War songs, I'm inviting all of you to contribute some numbers of your own. If you play an instrument, like piano or violin, I have sheet music for Civil War tunes that you can play for us. Any dancers in the class could do a Civil War dance. And someone could recite a Civil War poem, or Lincoln's Gettysburg Address."

Ricky called out, "Lance plays the violin."

Amanda knew that James played the violin, too. She had seen him carrying a violin case to school on instrumental music days.

"Meghan and I can do an Irish dance," Beth offered. She leaned over Amanda to flash Meghan a confident smile.

Amanda didn't play an instrument or dance. No one in their family was musical, except for her father, and until recently he hadn't touched his saxophone in years. Her mother always used to make sarcastic comments when he played it. Amanda wouldn't mind reciting a poem for the concert. She wondered if Mrs. Angelino would let her write her own poem, or if she had to use an old-time poem from an anthology.

"You'll have one week to work on your numbers. Then we'll have auditions. I know it will be hard for me to make my selections with so much talent in this class! But we'll want to pick only the very best numbers to perform for your parents."

If Amanda were picking the very best music for the program, she'd leave out "Goober Peas." Or at least she'd put Ricky in the back row, behind someone very tall.

After school, Amanda met Beth by the coatracks so they could start walking home to Beth's house together. Beth was busy talking to Meghan, probably about their Civil War dance.

"Meghan's coming with us today," Beth told Amanda. She

didn't add, "Okay?" If she had, of course Amanda would have said, "Sure." What else could she have said, with Meghan standing right there? But it would have been polite at least to ask.

"Wait! I have an idea!" Meghan said as they headed out the door.

"What?" Amanda asked.

"The O'Reilly jig. The one we did last year, for the April recital?"

Amanda felt foolish for having thought Meghan had been speaking to both of them.

"It's pretty long," Beth said. "I think Mrs. Angelino's going to pick short pieces, to get more people on the program."

"How about—what was the name of that one? The one that goes like this?" Meghan started dancing right in the middle of the sidewalk in front of the school.

Amanda tried to catch Beth's eye, to see if Beth was as irritated as she was, but Beth shrugged off her backpack, dropped it on the sidewalk, and started dancing, too. Amanda was getting her own private Irish jig concert, for an audience of one. Except that she didn't think Beth and Meghan even remembered she was there.

Finally the dance was over. Amanda thought of clapping, but she knew it would seem sarcastic.

"That's it!" Beth said. "It's perfect."

"Did people do Irish dancing during the Civil War?" Amanda couldn't resist asking.

Beth shrugged. "Probably."

"It's not like Mrs. Angelino is going to check," Meghan said.

Didn't *they* want to check? Amanda had checked whether people sent telegrams during the Civil War. She had researched the picnicking during the First Battle of Bull Run. She still hadn't checked about hay versus alfalfa, but she would.

"We can practice it more when we get home," Beth said. "I have the DVD of the concert. We can watch it to make sure we have all the steps right."

So first Amanda had to watch Beth and Meghan dancing; now she'd have to watch them watching a DVD of themselves dancing.

"What about the math homework?" Amanda asked.

Meghan rolled her eyes at Beth. Even though Amanda had tried to roll her own eyes at Beth a few minutes ago, she felt her cheeks flush with anger.

"We only have ten problems," Meghan said. "It'll take five minutes, tops."

Five minutes for Meghan, maybe. Not five minutes for Amanda. Amanda couldn't do the math homework without Beth's help. But she wasn't going to ask for it in front of Meghan.

Her eyes sent a pleading signal to Beth.

Beth looked away.

"Actually," Amanda said, trying to keep her voice steady, "I just remembered that my mother told me to come home right away after school today." She tried to think of a plausible reason to add, but couldn't come up with one.

There was a long pause. Amanda knew that Beth knew that she was lying. She knew that Meghan didn't care whether she was lying or not.

"Okay," Beth said.

"See you tomorrow!" Meghan called out cheerfully.

Amanda gave a weak smile. Then she turned and walked toward home, alone.

On the computer in her mother's basement office, Amanda searched for "Irish dancing" and "Civil War." Right away she found a Web site about an Irish brigade celebrating Christmas during the Civil War by doing Irish jigs and reels. Then she searched for "hay" and "alfalfa" and found out that alfalfa was actually a kind of hay, and it was indeed grown in Maryland; there were whole Web sites for buying and selling it.

Should she call Beth and Meghan to tell them that they were right, after all? Maybe they had been secretly worried about whether their dance was historically accurate, and would appreciate the reassurance. And maybe the kind thoughtfulness of the call would make them feel sorry that they had gone off together without her.

Beth picked up the phone. At least she wasn't too busy jigging with Meghan to hear the phone ring.

"Hi, Beth, it's Amanda."

"Hi." Beth didn't sound particularly friendly.

"I just want to let you and Meghan know that I checked on the Internet about Irish dancing during the Civil War, and it's fine, they did have Irish dancing back then."

"You checked on the Internet?" Beth sounded suspicious rather than grateful, as if Amanda had been trying to prove them wrong instead of right.

"Well, I was checking some other stuff, for my Polly diary. I just thought you and Meghan would want to know."

"Sure," Beth said. "Thanks."

Amanda waited to see if Beth would ask her if she could come over now to join them. Beth didn't.

"So, bye," Amanda said.

"Bye," Beth said. And that was that.

Annoyed with herself for calling, Amanda dragged out her math homework. Then, before she could talk herself out of it, she called James.

"Hi, James. It's Amanda. MacLeish. From school." As if he knew lots of different Amanda MacLeishes with high, nervous voices.

"Hey," James said. His hello sounded a lot friendlier than Beth's.

Amanda hesitated. Then James said, "Math homework, right?"

"Well . . . do you mind?"

"No, it's fine. Let me get my book."

As before, James was better at explaining the problems than even Beth or Mr. Abrams.

"You should be a math teacher," Amanda told him.

"I want to be a scientist."

"Like Albert Einstein," Amanda said.

"That's right," James said. "Just call me Al, for short." Amanda could hear the grin in his voice.

"Are you going to play the violin for the concert?" Amanda asked.

"I'm going to audition."

"How long have you been playing violin?"

"Since first grade. I take lessons at the Arts Center. What about you? Are you going to try out for the concert? Aren't you a dancer?"

"No, that's Beth." *And her new best friend, Meghan.*

"You could read one of your Polly entries."

"Everybody has Civil War diary entries."

"Not as good as yours."

Amanda wondered if James could hear her own grin in the moment of pleased, shy silence before she said, "Thanks."

"Gotta go," James said.

When Amanda hung up, her heart felt less bruised and sore than it had all day. And now it was time to visit Polly.

Dear Diary,

I fell asleep in the alfalfa, and when I woke up, the wagon had stopped, and the farmer, Mr. Porter, was offering me some water from his earthenware jug and a handful of goober peas from a burlap sack.

"Have some," he said.

"Thank you, sir," I said. "Goober peas are delicious."

We both sat eating them for a while, tossing the shells into the grass by the side of the dusty road.

"You don't sound like a boy," Mr. Porter said.

I had forgotten to make my voice low when I thanked him for the goober peas. Quickly I reached up to make sure my cap was still on my head, covering my hair. I could feel a few strands falling down in back and tried to stuff them up under the cap again without being too obvious.

"Sometimes my voice comes out high," I said, making it low again.

We crossed the river over to Virginia on a ferry. The closer we got to the hospital, the more my heart filled with hope. Maybe I'd see Jeb today. He'd be lying in the hospital bed, a bandage on his forehead and his arm in a sling. "Hi, Polly," he'd say. "I knew you'd come."

I lay on the alfalfa watching the clouds go by, white puffy clouds like balls of cotton. I thought about the slaves picking cotton on a hot day like this one, with no break for water or goober peas. Why didn't Jeb see that the South was wrong to have slav-

ery? Slaves were just as smart as the people who owned them, maybe smarter. If they weren't slaves, they could be great scientists, or math teachers, or violinists.

The hospital didn't look like a hospital at all to me. It was a cluster of ragged, dirty tents at the edge of a battlefield. I don't know which battlefield. Maybe it was Bull Run. It looked different without the armies shooting and screaming and bleeding and dying. But if I closed my eyes, I could still see the smoke from the cannons and hear the neighs of frightened horses trying to gallop away.

There was a main tent and some other smaller tents. We went inside the main tent. I hoped there would be someone I could ask about Jeb. But there was no one sitting by the door to answer questions.

"What do we do now?" I asked Mr. Porter.

"I guess we look," he said.

We walked up one row of beds and down another, looking at each soldier to see if he was Jeb. Some of them were missing legs. Some of them were missing arms. The worst one was missing part of his face, but his hair was black, not red, so I knew it couldn't be Jeb.

At one bed, the nurse was covering the soldier with a sheet. I knew what it meant when she drew the sheet up over his face. He was dead. I had to check to make sure it wasn't Jeb.

I prayed as hard as I could. Then she pulled the sheet back so I could see. It wasn't Jeb. It was some other girl's brother. I couldn't even feel glad.

Without thinking, I pulled off my cap and placed it over my heart.

"We'd best go now—Paul," Mr. Porter said gently.

I followed him back to the wagon, my cap hanging from my hand. Then, too late, I remembered my hair, falling down over my shaking shoulders.

10

Amanda's father had moved out almost three weeks ago, and the house still felt empty without him. Amanda caught herself listening for signs of him, the way her tongue would keep poking into the hole in her mouth where a loose tooth used to be. But her tongue would accept the lost tooth after a day or two, even after a few hours. It was harder to let go of a father.

Steffi didn't seem to miss him. At least, she didn't say she did. Of course, Amanda didn't say that she did, either. She was afraid to say anything about him to Steffi. Ever since the rainy-day visit to their dad's apartment, her sister had been distant and unfriendly. Amanda couldn't believe Steffi was still cross because Amanda and their father had walked in the rain without her. But it took so little to make Steffi turn sulky these days.

Their mother seemed to miss him more than Steffi did.

Maybe she just missed the things he used to do in the house. When the paper in the printer in her basement office jammed, she tried for half an hour to pry the stuck piece of paper from the rollers, but couldn't do it. Steffi and Amanda were summoned to help, but Amanda's tugs were no more effective than her mother's, and Steffi refused even to try.

"It's not going to come out, Mom," she said.

"I thought kids today were supposed to be technological whizzes. All my friends' children are upgrading the software on their parents' computers and teaching their parents how to design their own Web pages."

"Not us," said Steffi.

In the end, their mother had a friend from work stop by one evening to do it, a male friend.

Their father would have had the printer unjammed in two minutes.

Then, on Saturday morning, Amanda woke up to hear a muffled scream from the kitchen. She ran downstairs. Steffi didn't. Either she was still sleeping—Steffi was the soundest sleeper in the family—or she didn't think it was especially important to see what their mother could be screaming about.

Amanda's mother was sitting in a kitchen chair, crying. "I can't do it," she said.

"Do what?"

She pointed to the open pantry door. Uneasy, Amanda started toward it.

"Don't. Don't go in there."

For a fleeting second, Amanda expected to see a body lying on the pantry floor. Maybe it was an intruder, an armed burglar, who had broken into the house to prey on a woman alone with two helpless daughters, but had somehow gotten himself killed instead. Or it could be her dad, felled by a heart attack brought on by fighting with her mother.

At first Amanda didn't notice anything. Then she saw it: a dead mouse.

She forced back a scream of her own. *It's just a mouse,* she tried to tell herself. But the deadness of it, lying there . . .

Amanda thought she might be sick. Swallowing hard, she dropped into the chair next to her mother's.

Steffi appeared in the doorway. "What is it? What's going on?"

Amanda wasn't going to let Steffi have the shock of finding it herself.

"It's a . . . dead mouse," she whispered.

Steffi screamed louder than their mother had before. Up she jumped onto a chair, as if the mouse were going to come back to life and dart across her bare, unprotected feet.

Suddenly their mother started laughing. After a startled pause, Amanda and Steffi joined in. It was too ridiculous, all of them cowering before the small corpse of a poor, perfectly harmless mouse. Amanda even liked mice, in stories at least. The City Mouse and the Country Mouse. The mice who turned into Cinderella's horses. Stuart Little!

When they had finished laughing, there was a long moment of silence.

"Should I call your dad?" their mother asked. "He's heading out on a business trip to Atlanta, but I don't think he's left yet."

Yes! Call him and tell him you want him to move home again.

"No," Steffi said, sounding annoyed. "What about the guy who fixed the printer?"

"Tom? I'm not going to call him every time I have some little problem."

Was a dead mouse a little problem or a big problem? It would be a little problem for Polly Mason. Living on a farm, Polly probably got rid of dead mice all the time, dead rats even. She'd pick them up and carry them outside and fling them away like the shells of so many cracked goober peas.

"I'll do it," Amanda said in a brave voice.

Steffi stared, looking impressed.

"Oh, honey, do you think you could?" their mother asked.

Amanda nodded.

"Use a plastic bag. One of the bags from the newspaper."

Polly would have done it without a plastic bag. But the plastic bag was a good idea. Like a dog walker cleaning up after her puppy, Amanda slipped the bag over her hand to form a plastic glove. Then she walked into the pantry, picked up the mouse, and quickly turned the plastic bag inside out over him, to create a small see-through shroud. Ta-da!

"Where should I put him?"

"Just put him outside in the trash can. It gets picked up on Monday."

That was all the funeral the mouse received. If Amanda hadn't borrowed Polly's bravery, their mom might have called their dad, despite Steffi's sneers, and they might have made up, and Amanda might have had two parents living in the same house again. But she still felt good about what she had done. It always felt good to do something you never dreamed you'd be able to make yourself do.

Amanda's mother was out all afternoon showing houses to clients. Tanya was over, watching TV in the family room with Steffi. Amanda could hear snippets of their conversation as she fixed herself a snack in the kitchen. Apparently Mike Weil liked another girl now, Sydney somebody. Tanya was asking Steffi for advice on how to get him back.

"Don't chase him," Steffi said. "The more you chase after a boy, the faster he runs away. It's like animal instinct or something, predator and prey. And whatever you do, don't let him see you cry. Boys can't stand being around girls who cry."

Amanda couldn't quite catch what Steffi said next, but the basic idea seemed to be to create elaborate strategies for Tanya to show Mike how little she cared.

Amanda half wanted to call Beth, but Beth was probably spending the afternoon with Meghan. Amanda wasn't going to chase after Beth any more than Tanya was going to chase after Mike Weil.

She thought about writing more Polly, but she didn't know what should happen next. It seemed boring to have Polly and Mr. Porter keep going to a bunch of hospitals and not finding Jeb. And if they did find him, the main story of the diary would be over. So instead Amanda read a Betsy-Tacy book. It was comforting to have the company of a family as loving and happy as Betsy's. Amanda loved how Mr. Ray invited all Betsy's friends to their house on Sunday nights for his famous onion sandwiches.

At six o'clock, Amanda's mother came home. Tanya's stepdad had picked her up half an hour earlier.

"What do you girls want to do for dinner?"

"Pizza," Steffi said.

"We could have onion sandwiches," Amanda suggested.

"Onion sandwiches?" Steffi and their mother asked together. It was plain that they had never read the Betsy-Tacy books.

"You slice the onions really thin, and put on salt and pepper."

The sandwiches sounded so good in the books, but Amanda had to admit they didn't sound all that appealing in real life. They wouldn't taste the same without the Ray family gathered around the piano, linking arms and singing.

Dinner ended up being soup from a can, with a thrown-together salad. "Pizza isn't cheap," their mother said, "now that we have to pay the bills for two households."

Amanda wondered what their dad was having. He had never done any cooking. Maybe he was heating up his own can of soup in one of the shiny, new-looking pans that came with his furnished apartment. Unless he had already left on his trip.

As she was ladling the soup, their mother said, "I've been thinking that we should consider getting a cat."

Amanda's eyes met Steffi's. She knew Steffi wanted a cat as much as she did. If their father hadn't been allergic, they would have had a cat long ago.

"It would take care of the mice problem," their mother went on.

Amanda didn't know what to say. Nothing could be sweeter than curling up to write a Polly diary entry with a purring cat for company. Except for writing a Polly diary entry while hearing a dad downstairs whistling in the kitchen.

"Let's get a kitten," Steffi urged. "Can we pick one out at the Humane Society tomorrow? We don't have to visit Dad because he's away on that business thing."

"Kittens are too much work," said their mother. "But we can go there tomorrow to see what they have. It's good to make a couple of visits, so we can be sure of what we want."

"Can I bring Tanya?"

"Sure. Amanda, do you want to ask Beth?"

Amanda shook her head. It was all happening too fast.

After dinner, she and Steffi loaded the dishwasher while their mom checked her e-mail.

Amanda carried the three soup bowls over from the table. Three soup bowls, not four. Carefully she set each bowl on the top rack. With only one person gone, there should have been almost as many dishes as before, but the dishwasher was practically empty. Her father must have used more dishes than the rest of the family put together.

"Dad can't come back if we get a cat," Amanda said, as if Steffi didn't know that as well as she did.

"I don't think Dad's coming back."

Someone had finally said it.

"The chain on the door? You heard what he told us, that he was sick from the crab sandwich. There wasn't any lady there, after all."

"Amanda." Steffi put so much tenderness in the name that the tears welled up in Amanda's eyes.

"That's what Dad said!"

"Yes." Steffi looked away. "That's what Dad said."

July 29, 1861

Dear Diary,

Well, when Mr. Porter saw my hair, he knew I wasn't a boy.

"Your name isn't really Paul, is it?" he asked then.

"No, sir. It's Polly, Polly Mason."

"A big city in wartime is no place for a girl," he said.

I put my cap back on and stuffed my hair underneath it. "That's why I'm a boy."

I waited a minute. Mr. Porter looked like he didn't know what to do. Then he laughed. "Let's go, Paul," he told me.

We went outside, and I climbed up onto the wagon.

"Let's head back to Washington," Mr. Porter said. "We can check at the hospital there."

I lay on the alfalfa and stared at the sky some more. Now the clouds looked less like cotton balls and more like cats. One white cloud looked a lot like Whitie. A dark cloud looked sort of like Blackie. Do you think Whitie and Blackie miss me?

Diary, this is how we got Whitie and Blackie.

Betsy—my best friend, remember?—had a cat, but we didn't. Mother said we didn't need any more animals. We already had one dog, two horses, three cows, four sheep, and five chickens. Thomas said, "If we have all those other animals, why not have one more?" Jeb drew pictures of a cat in the dirt with a stick. Then he drew words coming out of the cat's mouth: "I want to live in your house," the words said. Mother pretended not to see the pictures. She walked right over them when she went outside to hang the wash on the clothesline.

Then I had an idea. At night before I went to bed, I left a little piece of cheese on the kitchen table. In the morning, the cheese was gone, and I saw a mouse running across the floor. Some people are afraid of mice, but not me. I throw away dead mice all the time.

The next night, I left two little pieces of cheese on the table. That morning, I saw two mice running across the floor.

When I left out three pieces of cheese, and three mice came, Mother saw them, too. She chased them away with a broom, but they kept coming back day after day.

Mother went to get the cheese. It was all gone.

"Who has been eating all this cheese?" Mother asked.

"Mice like cheese," I said, as innocent as can be.

"I guess we need a cat," Mother said.

"Hooray!" Thomas, Jeb, and I all shouted.

Betsy's cat had just had kittens. Mother sent us to Betsy's house to pick out a kitten for us to keep. They were so cute, dear Diary. One was black, one was white, one was gray, one was orange, and one was all different colors mixed together.

It was hard to pick. We wanted all five, but Mother had said one.

Jeb liked Whitie the best. Thomas liked Blackie the best.

"Which one do you like best?" they asked me.

I looked at Thomas holding Blackie and Jeb holding Whitie. If I said Blackie, Jeb would be sad. If I said Whitie, Thomas would be sad. If I picked a different cat, they both would be sad.

"Let's take both," I said.

So we did. At first Mother was angry, but she couldn't stay angry for long because Blackie and Whitie were so adorable, and after that no more cheese was eaten by the mice.

I know, Diary. Thomas got Blackie, and Jeb got Whitie, and I didn't get any cat for myself. But then my brothers left, and I have both cats now, Blackie and Whitie.

I love our cats, dear Diary. But I would much rather have my brothers.

11

"If we get a cat, you girls are responsible for cleaning the litter box," their mother said as they drove on Sunday afternoon to the Humane Society.

"At Tanya's house, her mother pays her to do it, a dollar a day," Steffi pointed out. Tanya hadn't ended up coming, after all; she had plans with another friend.

"Does Tanya pay her mother for cleaning the house, cooking the meals, doing the laundry, and driving her to school?" their mother asked.

"It's not the same thing. Tanya's mother likes to clean and cook and do laundry."

Their mother laughed.

Steffi didn't look amused. "She does! And kids don't want to go to school. It's the parents who want us to. So they should drive us there."

Amanda wanted to go to school. Last summer she had made a chart at the start of August, crossing off the days until school would begin, something she hadn't admitted to Beth and would never admit to Steffi. She had a feeling that James liked school, too.

They pulled into the parking lot at the shelter. Inside, a teenaged boy was sitting at the front desk. With a friendly smile, he looked up from his computer monitor.

"What can I do for the three of you?" The boy was looking straight at Steffi.

"We want to see your cats," her mother said. "Remember, girls, we're not getting a cat today. We're just seeing what's available."

"Right." Steffi grinned at Amanda. The boy grinned, too.

"The cat room is straight ahead," the boy told them. "Take your time, wander around. If you see a cat you're interested in, let me know, and I'll bring him to you in our family meeting room at the end of the hall. And if you have any questions, just holler. I'm Ben."

Amanda was ready to go, but Steffi held back.

"Do you have any favorites?" she asked Ben.

"They're all my favorites. Though I'm really a dog person."

"Do you have a dog? At home?"

Who cared whether this boy had a dog or not? The real question was whether Amanda and Steffi were going to get a cat. Then Amanda recognized the look on Steffi's face. Steffi looked the way Tanya did when she talked about Mike Weil. And Ben seemed in no hurry to get back to whatever he had been doing on the computer.

"I have two," he said. "A black Lab and a golden retriever."

"Can we look at dogs, too?" Steffi asked her mother.

"You can *look* at whatever you want. But we're not even going to *think* about getting anything but a cat."

"Have fun looking," Ben said with another smile. This time the smile seemed to be directed especially at Steffi.

The first cage they examined had three kittens in it, adorable little ginger-colored furballs. One was asleep, but the other two were tumbling about in play. Amanda yearned to pick up all three and cuddle them.

"No kittens," their mother reminded them.

The cat in the second cage was ten years old, according to the information card hanging from the cage.

"Too old," Steffi said.

Another cat's card said he had been brought to the shelter because of problems using the litter box.

"That would be a no," Steffi said.

Amanda felt her chest tighten. What if nobody wanted an older cat, or a cat who couldn't use the litter box correctly, and those cats had to spend the rest of their lives in a little wire cage? Or be put to sleep—killed—because nobody wanted them? She wished she could take them all to Polly's farm. Even if Polly's mother wouldn't let them live in the house, they could sleep in the barn, fatten themselves on field mice, and curl up in the alfalfa warmed by the afternoon sun.

"Maybe we could teach him to use the litter box," Amanda suggested.

Her mother shook her head.

Steffi began to look a little more interested. "We could ask Ben for tips on how to do it," she suggested. But their mother had already started down the second row of cages.

Then they found her: a mostly orange cat with some tan stripes, one year old, brought to the shelter yesterday because her owner was moving to a no-pets apartment. "Sweet and affectionate," her information card said.

Steffi left to get Ben, and the two returned to the cat room together. Ben was tall, a whole head taller than Steffi, but he didn't look that much older—maybe fifteen.

Ben took the cat out of her cage, showing his obvious skill in handling animals. His manner with the cat was confident yet gentle.

In the family meeting room, Amanda and their mother claimed the couch, leaving another chair for Steffi. Steffi chose to remain standing next to Ben.

"I'll leave you alone with her to get acquainted," Ben said. He set the cat down on the floor and left, shutting the door behind him. Amanda could sense Steffi's disappointment.

At first the cat wandered around the room, in and out of the chair legs, brushing up against their ankles. Then she looked at Amanda and gave a plaintive meow. Amanda patted her lap, and the cat sprang onto it with one graceful leap, settled herself there, and began purring. Steffi perched on the arm of the couch and reached over to pet her. The cat kept on purring.

"So much for just looking today," Amanda's mother said ruefully. "What should we name her?"

Steffi stroked the tip of the cat's nose. "Velvet?"

"Velvet is usually black," Amanda pointed out. She tried to think of a Civil War name, but most Civil War names were better for a boy cat: Lincoln, Grant, Gettysburg. Maybe Goober, for Goober Peas?

"How about Peanut?"

"She's sort of peanut-colored," their mother said.

"Peanuts are hard, not soft," Steffi objected.

"Peanut butter is soft," Amanda said. "That could be her full name, Peanut Butter, Peanut for short."

Steffi ran to tell the good news to Ben, and he returned to carry Peanut Butter back to her cage, where she would have to wait a few minutes longer. Their mother paid Peanut Butter's adoption fees and filled out the paperwork while Amanda and Steffi chose a litter box, bag of kitty litter, food bowl and water bowl, sack of dry food and cans of wet food, brush, feather-tipped cat tease, and catnip-filled mouse.

"Are you all set?" Ben asked as they piled their purchases on his desk.

"Is there anything else you think she needs?" Steffi asked.

"Nope. The main thing is a lot of love, and I know you'll

give her that. Call me here at the shelter if you have any questions or concerns once you get her home. I'm Ben," he told them again.

"Thanks for all your help, Ben," their mother said.

"Thanks," Steffi echoed. "I'm Steffi," she added.

"Steffi," he repeated, as if to make sure to remember her name.

Amanda knew Steffi was trying to think of something else to say, but their mother was already maneuvering Peanut's carrier out the door. So with one last wave to Ben, Steffi turned and followed.

Miserable meows came from Peanut's cardboard carrier all the way home. When they opened the box in the living room, she jumped out and darted under the sofa to hide.

"Cats do that," their mother said. "It takes them a while to get used to new surroundings. When she comes out from under there, she'll be so dirty we'll have to give her a new name. Dust Bunny. Or Blackie."

"Can Tanya come over to see her?"

"Let her get used to us first for a day or two. This is a big adjustment for a little cat. And then, of course, Tanya and Beth can come. Amanda, I haven't seen Beth for ages—it must be weeks now. Is she still so busy with her Irish dancing?"

Amanda nodded. Even busier, now that Beth and Meghan were working together on their jig for the Civil War concert auditions.

"Tell Beth I miss her."

"Okay," Amanda said, even though she knew she wouldn't.

Peanut didn't come out from under the couch all afternoon. Amanda began to wonder if she would ever come out. Every hour or so, Amanda would crouch down on the floor and peer under the couch to make sure Peanut was still there and still breathing, and she'd see Peanut's green eyes staring.

"Peanut," Amanda called softly. "Come out, Peanut Butter, we're not going to hurt you."

"Do you think we should call Ben?" Steffi asked. "He said to call him if we had any problems."

"Maybe." It *was* odd that a cat who had been so friendly at the shelter would turn so shy and standoffish.

Steffi made the call from her cell phone, upstairs, so Amanda couldn't hear the conversation. When Steffi came back downstairs, she was beaming.

"He's a sophomore at Mount Vincent High. He already plays on the varsity soccer team. He doesn't get paid to work at the Humane Society; he does it as a volunteer. He's been doing it for two years now."

"What did he say about Peanut?"

"Oh, he said just to be patient."

And by eight o'clock, when Amanda's dad was due to

make his evening phone call, Peanut had emerged from hiding, had eaten and drunk from her new bowls, had used the litter box for the first time, and was back in Amanda's lap, purring as contentedly as before.

The phone rang promptly at eight. Amanda's dad was late for lots of things, but never for the phone call, even when he was off in Atlanta. Amanda answered the phone.

"Hi, Mandy, what's up?"

Should she tell him? She couldn't not tell him something so important and exciting, but he had to know what it meant, that the family that could never get a cat because of the father's allergies had a cat now.

"We got a cat."

There was a silence.

Amanda filled it. "We're calling her Peanut. For Peanut Butter. She's not a special breed or anything. Just a regular cat. She's one year old."

Her dad still hadn't spoken.

"She's on my lap now. Maybe if I hold the phone by her head, you can hear her purring."

Amanda held the phone down so that Peanut could purr into it. It was better than listening to the sound of her dad saying nothing. "Did you hear her?"

"That's fine, Mandy," he finally said. "I know you girls have wanted a cat for a long time. Is your mother around? I'd like to talk to her."

"I'll go get her."

Reluctantly, Amanda tipped Peanut out of her lap and called down the stairs to her mother's office. "Dad's on the phone! He wants to talk to you."

She listened into the receiver until she heard her mother pick up. Then, even though she knew it was wrong, she didn't hang up the phone, but stood there listening.

"Amanda tells me you got a cat."

"And?"

"I thought you wanted to try to work things out."

Her mother laughed, a hard, bitter, mirthless chuckle. "It takes two people to work things out, you know."

"So now if I move back, you'll have to get rid of the cat, and break the girls' hearts, and it will be all my fault, just like everything else?"

"You said it, not me."

"It takes two to work things out; it also takes two to get them broken in the first place."

"I can't believe you have the nerve to say that to me. After what you—"

"I told you, nothing happened until you got all upset for no reason at all."

"But it didn't turn out to be for no reason at all, did it?"

"Listen. I called to talk to the girls. Put Steffi on, will you?"

Amanda clicked off the phone. Her mother came upstairs, her face rigid with suppressed anger. "Amanda, go tell Steffi that Dad's on the phone."

Amanda did. She heard Steffi's side of the conversation.

"Yeah, a really cute cat . . . Yeah . . . Well, Amanda picked out the name . . . Okay . . . Talk to you tomorrow. Bye, Dad."

She hadn't told him anything about meeting Ben. Maybe that wasn't the kind of thing Steffi would tell anyone but Tanya.

Amanda went into her room and lay down on her bed. Her mother had said that it took two people to work things out, but Amanda knew that the whole point of getting Peanut was to let their father know that things were never going to work out. Her father had sounded as if he might move back someday, and her mother had as much as said it was never going to happen.

Peanut jumped up on the bed beside her. It was amazing how high a little cat could leap in one bound.

"Go away," Amanda said. But even as she spoke, she drew Peanut closer and pressed her cheek against her cat's soft fur.

July 30, 1861

Dear Diary,

Mr. Porter and I camped last night by the side of the road. He slept in his bedroll under a tree, and I slept in the alfalfa in the wagon. He gave me a roll and some cheese for breakfast. Then we drove into Washington. The country road turned into a paved city street. There were people and horses everywhere. Mr. Porter pulled up in front of a large brick building.

Inside we met a nurse. "Hello," the nurse said. "My name is Clara Barton."

"Hello," I said. "My name is Paul Mason. I'm looking for my brother, Jeb Mason."

The next moment was the terrible one. What if Clara Barton told me that my brother was dead? I hadn't checked the newspapers since I ran away from home. Maybe Jeb was dead by now.

"Jeb Mason," Clara Barton said. "The name sounds familiar."

"He had—he has—red hair and freckles. He's only fifteen, even though he tries to act older."

"Yes, he was here," Clara Barton said. "But I'm sure he said he had a younger sister, not a younger brother. He kept talking about her. 'Tell Polly I'm all right,' he kept saying."

I started to cry then. I couldn't stop myself. I pulled off my cap. "I'm Polly, ma'am."

Clara Barton hugged me. "You brave girl, to come all this way to find your brother. When this war is over, many people will remember the bravery of the women."

I thought Clara Barton was brave, too, to nurse sick and dying men so far from home.

But I still didn't know what I had come to find out.

"Where is Jeb now? How badly was he wounded? Is he going to be okay?"

Clara Barton looked sad. "He lost his arm. But the doctors thought he would recover. He was moved to another hospital."

She told Mr. Porter where it was. I couldn't listen. I felt like throwing up at the thought of Jeb without an arm, his arm not broken, soon to be mended, healing in a sling, but gone forever. Jeb with an empty sleeve to his jacket for the rest of his life.

But at least he is alive, dear Diary. At least my one-armed brother is alive.

12

During diary-sharing time on Thursday, Mr. Abrams asked Ricky to take a turn reading what he had written. Amanda hadn't heard any of Ricky's entries yet. Lance waved his hand every time to share more about his slave boy, Jonah, but Ricky never volunteered.

"I'm Abraham Lincoln," Ricky said.

Everybody laughed. It was hard to think of anyone less presidential than Ricky.

"Go ahead, Mr. President," Mr. Abrams said. "I know this terrible Civil War must be much on your mind these days."

Ricky scowled down at his crumpled piece of paper. " 'Dear Diary. Today was a big battle between two ships. One ship was the *Monitor*. One ship was the *Merrimack*. They were both made of iron. I'm surprised they didn't sink. How can an iron boat float? The battle was long. Neither side won. It was boring. I hate being President. The end.' "

"Okay," Mr. Abrams said with his usual kindly grin. "Comments for Ricky?"

"I think he needs to explain more why the battle was so important," James said. "I mean, this was the most famous naval battle of the Civil War. I can't believe anyone could think it was a boring battle. Especially the President, the commander in chief. If the *Monitor* had won, it would have meant certain defeat for the Union."

"What do you think, Ricky?" Mr. Abrams asked. "Do you want to add a little more about why this particular battle was so significant?"

"No."

"And, James," Mr. Abrams added, "remember we always want to start by offering some positive comment about everybody's writing."

He paused expectantly to give James the chance to say something nice about Ricky's entry.

"Well, I guess it's interesting that he made Lincoln say he doesn't like being President. But he doesn't tell us why."

"Any other comments for Ricky?"

"I liked it," Lance said, glaring at James. "Why *didn't* those ships sink? Isn't iron heavier than water?"

"That's a good question. Does anyone know the answer?"

James was the only one to raise his hand. "They were iron*clad* ships, not solid iron. And look at the shape of a ship. A ship is a hollow shell with lots of air in it."

"Thank you, James. Who else hasn't read?" Mr. Abrams asked. "Meghan, we haven't heard from you for a while."

In Meghan's diary entry, her Northern girl, Martha, was helping to hide a slave family who had arrived covered by a load of hay on the back of a farmer's wagon. Amanda had to admit that Meghan's entries were good. She made sure to be the first to offer a compliment after Meghan finished reading.

"I liked how you ended in an exciting place, so we don't know if the slaves got captured or not."

"Thanks," Meghan said.

Amanda didn't add that Meghan's girl shouldn't have been dancing an Irish jig on her way to the barn to check on the slaves there. She would have crept along silently, not stomping away on her hard wooden clogs.

"We have time for one more," Mr. Abrams said.

"Amanda's," Beth urged. "Let's hear Amanda's."

Was Beth trying to pretend that nothing had changed and that they were still best friends? Or did she just want to avoid being called on herself, or made to listen to Lance's pathetic Jonah?

"By popular demand," Mr. Abrams said, smiling at Amanda.

She read her cat entry. The others clapped when she was done.

"You must be a cat person, Amanda. Do you have a cat?" Mr. Abrams asked.

"No," Beth answered for her. "She can't get a cat because her father's allergic."

"That's part of the joy of writing, then," Mr. Abrams said. "Our characters can have the experiences we would like to have, but can't, for one reason or another."

"Actually," Amanda blurted out, "we just got a cat. Last weekend. From the Humane Society."

"What's its name?" Meghan asked.

"What does it look like?" Lance asked.

"Peanut. She's orange and tan, sort of peanut-colored."

Amanda didn't let herself meet Beth's eyes.

"Your father can get a prescription to help him with his allergies," Mr. Abrams said. "And your vet can give you something to put in Peanut's food, too."

Or her father could move away and solve the problem altogether.

"All right, class, line up for music. Don't you have your concert auditions today? Good luck, everybody."

Amanda held back until Beth and Meghan were safely in line ahead of her. She would have told Beth about Peanut sooner, if Beth weren't spending every minute with Meghan these days. And if Beth weren't so happy all the time with her perfect parents and perfect house and perfect math homework and perfect farmers' market cheese and cider. Beth didn't want to know anything about Amanda's life anymore. Either Beth couldn't see how much pain Amanda was in, or she didn't care.

"My woman's soldier husband finally died," she heard Beth say to Meghan. "She's taking it really hard. 'No! No! My John dead? No! No!' "

Beth recited it as if it were funny, delivering the lines with exaggerated emotion, holding the back of her hand to her forehead. It wasn't funny to Amanda. What was a devastated widow supposed to say?

What was a heartbroken friend supposed to say?

★ ★ ★

Mrs. Angelino's smile was even wider and more enthusiastic than usual as she welcomed Amanda's class into the music room. "Boys and girls, I can't wait to see the wonderful talents you're ready to share at our Civil War program!"

The students sat themselves on the risers; Mrs. Angelino didn't separate Lance and Ricky this time. Maybe she thought they'd be too caught up in the excitement of the auditions to misbehave.

"All right. Who has an act to audition?"

About half the class raised their hands, including Amanda. She had written a Civil War poem to read. She wished she didn't have to recite it for the first time in front of the whole class. Sharing a poem was scarier than reading Polly entries.

Beth and Meghan went first. Beth handed Mrs. Angelino a CD of the music to play on the classroom CD player. "You have to imagine that we're wearing our Irish dancing costumes," Beth explained. "The dance looks a lot cooler when we're wearing our costumes."

Even without the costumes, the dance was spectacular. Amanda was torn between the pride she always felt when Beth danced well and jealousy at the way Beth and Meghan grinned triumphantly at each other when the dance was finished.

James performed next. His violin piece was the theme music from the Ken Burns Civil War series on TV; Amanda's class had watched a couple of the programs during social studies time over the past few weeks. James played flawlessly, and the piece was so sad and beautiful, so full of homesickness and sorrow, that tears stung Amanda's eyes. The violin sang Polly's feelings as she searched for Jeb, Polly's fears that Jeb and Thomas would never come home again. It sang Amanda's feelings that her father would never come home again, and that she would never again be friends with Beth.

Right after James came Lance. Lance didn't play as well as James, but he had obviously been taking violin lessons for a long time. Amanda couldn't tell what connection Lance's piece had with the Civil War. It sounded like a piece of classical music he had performed at a violin recital.

Mrs. Angelino kept her face expressionless as she made some marks on her clipboard. Lance seemed extremely pleased with himself as he returned to the risers. For a joke, Ricky had clapped his hands over his ears during Lance's piece, so Lance punched him in the shoulder, and Ricky punched him back.

"Lance, maybe you could make a better seating choice," Mrs. Angelino said wearily.

With his violin bow, Lance gave Ricky one last quick whack and then sat down next to Patrick.

Amanda waited for her turn to read while one girl played a pretty good Civil War–era waltz on the piano and another girl played Taps on the trumpet with a couple of painful squawks that made Ricky cover his ears again, this time in earnest.

"Amanda?" Mrs. Angelino looked her way.

"Mine is a poem." Amanda stood up in the front of the room, folded her hands behind her back, and recited:

"Polly's Lament
My brother Jeb fights for the South.
My brother Thomas, for the North.
I do not fight for either side.
I watch the soldiers marching forth.
What if a bullet shot by Jeb
Should strike Thomas in the heart?
What if a bullet shot by Thomas
Should strike Jeb like a poisoned dart?
How can I live without my brothers?
Why do they have to fight each other?"

Mrs. Angelino made more marks on her pad. Beth gave Amanda a thumbs-up. Amanda wished she had given Beth a thumbs-up after her dance. Why *did* brothers, or friends, or parents, have to fight each other?

"Thank you, boys and girls!" Mrs. Angelino said. "Now, if you're not picked for a special act, please don't be disappointed. The chorus is still the most important part of our show! I'll post the audition results on the music room door right after school."

★ ★ ★

When the final bell rang, Amanda held herself back from the crowd of kids shoving forward to see the list, kids from all three fifth-grade classes, not just from Amanda's.

"We got in!" Meghan called to Beth. "We're the only ones from our class!"

So that was that. Though Amanda couldn't believe that James hadn't been picked. If Amanda had picked only one act, it would have been James's haunting solo on the violin.

"No, wait," Meghan said. Amanda's heart skipped a beat. "James got in on his violin, and Amanda's poem got picked, too."

Amanda felt relieved. It wasn't so much that she wanted to read her poem on the program, but that she didn't want to be rejected, especially if Beth and Meghan had been chosen.

Ricky was standing closer to the list than Lance was.

"Did I get picked?" Lance yelled to him. He must not have heard Meghan's report. Though maybe Meghan had missed seeing Lance's name, if she had missed James and Amanda at first.

"Nope." Ricky pushed his way back out of the crowd. "Just the stupid Irish dance and Amanda's stupid poem and James's stupid violin."

Lance's face darkened with anger. "My mom told me they always pick the black kids, to make it look better."

Amanda saw James standing a bit apart from the crowd, like her—either too proud or too shy to elbow his way to the front of the line.

Lance strode over to James. "Congratulations, *Jonah*," he sneered.

Amanda couldn't believe the nastiness in Lance's voice. She had to speak up, to say something: *Lance, you can't talk to James like that; Lance, what you just said to James was racist and wrong.* Instead, she froze in horrified silence.

James clenched his fist, and for a moment Amanda thought there might be a fight between the two boys.

"Wait—James—don't—" she finally managed to blurt out.

James whirled around and gave her an angry look. He must have thought she was blaming him for reacting, instead of blaming Lance for starting it all.

Then, without a word, James turned and walked away.

Dear Diary,

When Mr. Porter and I came out of the hospital, I heard a band playing and saw a crowd gathered in the street.

"What's happening?" I asked him.

"It's the President!" he told me.

The President! Abraham Lincoln! I saw a tall, gaunt man with a stovepipe hat and a dark beard, looking exactly like the pictures I had seen, only sadder somehow.

I'm sad, too, so my heart went out to him. He didn't seem to like being President very much.

Mr. Porter and I joined the crowd waiting to hear Mr. Lincoln speak. Then the President stepped up onto a wooden crate and began.

"Four score and five years ago," he said, "the Union was founded, to give liberty and justice to all. To all," he repeated. And, dear Diary, he looked right at me.

"To this boy—what is your name, young man?"

Mr. Lincoln was speaking to me!

"It's Paul Mason, sir."

"The Union gives liberty and justice to boys like Paul."

Then he pointed to a black slave girl in the crowd. She was carrying some parcels for a grand white lady, all dressed up in a fancy dress with hoopskirts and a feathered bonnet. The lady must be the girl's owner.

"And you, young lady, what's your name?" Mr. Lincoln asked her.

At first the girl looked too shy and scared to speak. The lady gave her a mean look, as if she might beat the girl for daring to speak to someone as important as Mr. Lincoln. Then the girl whispered, "Susan, sir."

"The Union needs to give liberty and justice to girls like Susan."

The crowd cheered, except for the white lady, who looked meaner than ever. The meanness in her face made her ugly despite her velvet and satin gown. But she didn't turn and walk away. It was probably too exciting to see an actual President standing right in front of you.

"Come here, Paul and Susan," Mr. Lincoln said.

My heart pounded as I walked forward. Susan looked timidly at the white lady, but walked forward, too. I smiled at Susan. She smiled at me. I wondered if she knew that I was really a girl, like her. Not completely like her, because I am white and she is black. And I am free, and she is a slave.

But inside, she's free. Inside, we're just the same.

"This is what we're fighting for," Mr. Lincoln said. "For liberty and justice for Paul and Susan."

He stepped down from the wooden box. The speech was over. The band started playing again, "The Battle Hymn of the Republic," and everybody started singing, except for Susan's white lady, who yanked Susan's arm to lead her away.

I think that was a very good speech, dear Diary. Don't you?

13

To soothe her aching heart, Amanda had written her Polly diary entry as soon as she got home. But her heart still felt raw and bruised from what had happened at school.

She had to call James. She had to tell him that she was sorry for not speaking up to defend him after what Lance had said. That one word—*Jonah*—seemed to have struck James like a fist in the stomach. Her own stomach churned from pain for James and from guilt for doing nothing. She had stood there in silence, and James had seen her do it.

She forced herself to call James's number; no one answered. She didn't leave a message.

She tried again five minutes later, and five minutes after that.

"Were you calling Beth?" her mother asked, coming into the kitchen to make herself a cup of tea.

Amanda wished her mother would stop asking about

Beth. She didn't have to be friends with Beth for her whole life just to please her mother.

"Yes," Amanda lied. She put the phone down and walked to the window that looked out over the driveway where her dad's car wasn't parked anymore and might never be parked again. Remorse about James mixed with jealousy of Beth and the simmering anger at her mother that she had never yet expressed.

"Beth was out having fun with her *parents.*" Amanda didn't mean to say what she said next; it came rushing out in one great burst. "Beth's parents get along. They argue sometimes, like about global warming and things like that, but you can tell they don't hate each other. It's more like a game. But you and Dad—why can't you get along? Why does he have to live somewhere else?"

Her mother didn't answer right away. "It's complicated," she finally said.

"For you two, even a game isn't a game. You can't even play Monopoly without fighting."

"Maybe that's why we need to live apart."

That wasn't what Amanda had wanted her to say. She wanted her to say, "You're right, Amanda. I've been very silly quarreling with your dad over little things like a board game. Your dad can move back home now, and I'll never do it again."

"You think I'm to blame for everything, don't you?" her mother asked then.

Well, aren't you? "No." Amanda refused to give her mother the satisfaction of knowing she had read her unspoken thoughts so well.

The teakettle started to whistle. "Do you want any tea?" Amanda's mother asked gently.

Amanda accepted a steaming cup. She could tell her mother was trying to be friendly, and she didn't have the heart or stomach to quarrel anymore.

Amanda changed the subject. "At school today? A boy in my class said something racist to another boy. Lance did, to James."

"James is the black boy?"

"His dad is black, but his mom is white. I guess that makes him black. He looks black. Mrs. Angelino always smiles at him when she says anything nice about black people."

Her mother sighed. "Sometimes well-intentioned people can be the most insensitive of all."

"The worst part was—I was there when it happened, standing right next to them, and I wanted to say something to Lance, to tell him that he was wrong to say what he did— and I didn't. And when I finally started to say something, I think James thought I was criticizing *him*."

Her mother reached over and put her hand on Amanda's. Amanda didn't push it away.

"Don't be too hard on yourself, honey. Even a lot of adults have trouble speaking up when someone says something offensive—a racist joke, a sexist comment. Most people don't have the courage to say what needs to be said."

"But James is my friend. Well, sort of a friend. And I don't want to be like most people."

"So what are you going to do? To try to make things right?"

"I was going to call James and tell him I'm sorry."

"That's a good idea. I think that will mean a lot to him."

Amanda took a sip of her tea. It felt soothing to her throat, which was tight and sore from talking about her dad, and then about Lance and James. Telling her mother about Lance and James had helped. But she would still never forgive her mother for making her dad move away.

When the phone rang a few minutes later, Amanda's wild thought was that it might be James. Maybe his family had caller ID, so he'd know she had tried three times to call him—an embarrassing thought.

A boy's voice asked to speak to Steffi.

"Steffi!" Amanda called upstairs. She listened until she heard Steffi's "Hello?"

"Hey, Steffi, this is Ben. From the Humane Society."

Amanda hung up, gladness for Steffi easing some of her pain. Steffi had borrowed Tanya's cousin's high school yearbook from last spring and found three pictures of Ben in it: his class picture, his picture with the soccer team, and a picture of him clowning around in the cafeteria with two other guys. Copies of the pictures, made on their mother's office machine, had the place of honor on the bulletin board by Steffi's bed. After school yesterday, Steffi and Tanya had biked to the Humane Society, planning to pretend that Tanya wanted to adopt a dog, but Ben hadn't been there. Now he had actually called her on the phone.

Ten minutes later, Steffi appeared in the kitchen, her face radiant.

"That was Ben. He called to see how Peanut was adjusting. His dog Honey got sprayed by a skunk, and they had to wash her five times before the smell went away. Ben was the one who washed her. He told me his soccer team is playing on Saturday at eleven, and I can come to watch the game if I want."

Steffi scooped up Peanut, who was meowing around her feet. "I love you, I love you, I love you," she crooned to the cat, who accepted her hug for a moment, then squirmed to get down again.

From the phone upstairs, Amanda tried James's number once more. This time his mother answered.

"Is James there?"

"He's at his violin lesson, over at the Arts Center. He biked there right after school. He'll be finished around four-thirty. Can I give him a message?"

"Well—just tell him Amanda called, please."

Amanda hung up. Now James would think she had called about the math homework, and if she told him she was sorry, it would feel like something she stuck into the conversation to sound less self-centered: "I need you to help me with math again, and oh, while you're looking for your math book, I'm sorry I didn't stick up for you after what Lance said. So how *do* you multiply fractions?"

She checked her watch. It was four o'clock. She could bike to the Arts Center and probably catch James before he started home. She wanted to talk to him in person, before she saw him at school tomorrow.

Her mother gave her a quick hug when she told her where she was going.

"I'm proud of you, sweetie. Bike safely!"

The ride took only twenty minutes; Amanda pedaled her fastest to make sure she didn't miss James. Once she reached the Arts Center, she wasn't sure where to look for him, so she went inside to the main lobby, where the reception had been held after Beth's dance recital.

From down the corridor, she could hear the tinkle of a piano, the sweet sound of a saxophone, and a violin that might or might not be James's. Maybe she should start taking music lessons. She had thought once about learning to play the harp, but she knew she didn't have her father's musical talent. Too bad Amanda hadn't made Polly play the harp. It was too late to add that to Polly's story; now all Polly cared about was finding Jeb.

Amanda realized that the violin was silent. One of the music room doors opened, and James came into the corridor, violin case in hand. Amanda's heart thumped in her chest. It had been stupid to come. James probably had already forgotten about Lance's dumb insult. Now he'd have to remember it, and he'd blame Amanda for sticking her nose in his business, and get mad at her all over again.

James was walking toward her.

"Hi," Amanda said.

"What are you doing here?" He didn't sound angry now.

Should she pretend she was about to have her first harp lesson?

"Your mother told me you had your lesson."

"And?"

"I just wanted to tell you . . ."

James stared straight ahead. Amanda could see a muscle tightening in his cheek.

"James, I'm sorry about what Lance said. And I'm sorry I didn't say anything when he said it. I wanted to—I really did—but—I didn't. So I'm sorry. That's all. I came to tell you that I'm sorry."

James met her eyes. He didn't smile, but the corners of his mouth relaxed a little bit. "Thanks" was all he said.

Amanda wanted to say something more, but she didn't know what else to say. She gave a tentative smile.

"See you tomorrow," James said. He didn't return her smile.

Amanda felt her own hopeful smile fade as he turned and headed out the door.

Now she had to pedal home in the falling darkness. She

hated riding in the dark, even though her bike had a light on it. The sooner she left, the sooner she'd be home, but she lingered in the bright, warm lobby, rewriting the scene with James in her head so that it ended with one quick grin on his part. "Call me if you need help with the math homework," James would say. Then would come the friendly flash of his teeth, making everything between them right again.

There was no one else left in the lobby, except for a pretty blond woman in a dark coat, probably waiting for her child to finish a piano or sax lesson.

The walls of the lobby were hung with framed photographs. Amanda wandered past a few of them. One was a photo of a bunch of paper clips; another, of a bunch of thumbtacks. Amanda's favorite was a photo of old-fashioned buttons, of all shapes and sizes. Amanda loved buttons. Each one seemed to have a story to tell. She tried to pick out which buttons Polly might have on her best Sunday dress—plain white ones, most likely. The Masons didn't have money to spend on fancy buttons shaped like little carved wooden roses.

A music room door opened, and a man came out, carrying an instrument case. From a distance, he almost looked like her father, just back from his business trip.

The woman in the dark coat waved at him. He waved back, his face aglow with pleasure at the sight of her.

It *was* Amanda's father.

Amanda darted into the short hallway where the restrooms were. She couldn't let her father see her there. She couldn't let him know that she knew.

And she did know. The woman even had long blond hair and lipstick. So Steffi was right, right about everything. The separation wasn't their mother's fault; it was his fault. No wonder she had told him to go, to leave forever and never come back.

"Were you waiting long?" she heard her father ask.

"No, I've just been here a few minutes." The woman's voice was light and lilting. "How was your sax lesson?"

"Well, let's just say it's good I have a patient teacher."

He laughed, and the woman laughed, too. It had been months since Amanda last heard her parents laugh together.

She didn't hear what they said next, but she peeked back into the lobby as they were heading out the front door.

He stopped, and turned toward the woman, and cupped her face in his hands, and kissed her on the mouth.

Amanda turned away and gazed at the photo in front of her through a glassy film of tears. It was the thumbtack photograph. Every thumbtack in it was piercing right into her heart.

★ ★ ★

Amanda's chest burned as she pedaled the last block home in the darkness. Out of breath from climbing so hard and fast uphill, she gasped for air, but the cold breeze stung her lungs. She parked her bike in the garage and made her way into the kitchen, where her mother was stirring something on the stove.

"Amanda? I was getting worried."

Then her mother looked up and caught sight of her face. "What happened?"

Amanda couldn't answer.

"Did you have a close call on your bike?"

It was easier just to nod.

"Oh, honey, what happened?" Her mother drew her into a hug.

"This one car—it didn't have its lights on—and it came up so fast."

"Are you sure you're all right? Did you have your light on? And your helmet?"

Amanda nodded again.

"Did you find James?"

"Uh-huh. I told him I was sorry. I don't think it helped very much."

"I'm sure it did. You're shivering. Go to your room and put on something warmer, and I'll have supper on the table in fifteen minutes."

Upstairs, Amanda threw on a sweater and scribbled a Polly diary entry as fast as she could write, the words pouring out of her in a torrent. She had never needed Polly more.

Dear Diary,

I am so sad, dear Diary.

I am the saddest I have ever been in my life.

Have you ever had a terrible surprise? When something completely unexpected happened, and you had no idea what was coming until it was too late and it hit you smack in the face, like a cannonball blowing up right in front of you?

This is what happened to me.

I was still happy from seeing Mr. Lincoln and having him call me by name, even though he thought my name was Paul, not Polly. Seeing him be so kind to the slave girl, Susan, made me proud that he was my President. When he talked about this terrible war, it almost seemed worth fighting.

But I didn't think it was worth Jeb's arm. Was ending slavery worth someone's arm? Maybe, if you were the person who was the slave. Maybe not, if you were the person who lost the arm.

Jeb wasn't fighting to end slavery, anyway. He was fighting to keep slavery. Or at least for the South to have the right to decide whether or not to keep slavery. How could my own dear brother be so wrong about something so important? I wished he could have heard Mr. Lincoln speak about Susan. Maybe then he would understand.

"We'd best go now," Mr. Porter said.

I climbed back into the wagon. Just then a long row of wagons pulled up to the hospital, filled with more wounded soldiers. I watched as some men began carrying the soldiers on their canvas stretchers. What if Jeb was there and I missed seeing him, after coming so far?

"Please, sir, can we wait?" I asked Mr. Porter.

"These are recently wounded men, Polly," he told me. Sometimes he forgot to call me Paul. "Your brother isn't going to be here with them. He was wounded over a week ago."

"Maybe he went back to battle with one arm, and was wounded again, worse this time." A one-armed man could still fire a gun, I thought. Or hand a gun to someone else to fire.

For some reason I knew I had to stay.

Mr. Porter sighed. "All right, Polly."

I slid off the alfalfa and stood at the side of the wagon, watching as each stretcher passed by. It was like being in the hospital again, seeing men with no arms, no legs, no faces, covered with blood, some of them moaning, some of them screaming. It was so hard to keep looking, but I couldn't not look, either.

Another stretcher passed by, and my heart stopped.

It wasn't Jeb.

It was Thomas.

Thomas!

I hadn't checked the papers for the lists of dead and wounded since the day I saw Jeb's name. All I had thought of since then was finding Jeb. I had never even thought about Thomas.

"Thomas!"

The man—boy—on the stretcher turned toward me.

"Polly?"

Thomas, my bossy brother, my not-favorite brother, my brother who was *fighting to free Susan and all the other slaves*— Thomas looked at me. I knew he didn't know what I was doing there. And how could I tell him that I had searched everywhere to find Jeb, never thinking of him at all?

I reached out and took his hand. He still had a hand, but I didn't know how badly he was wounded. His face looked the same, though twisted with pain.

"Are you okay?" I asked him. It was a stupid question. Of course he wasn't okay, or he wouldn't be lying on a stretcher, being carried into an army hospital.

"No, Polly," he said. I had forgotten how gentle his voice could be.

"Go along, little boy," an army man told me. "This man is seriously wounded."

"I'm his sister," I said.

The man stared at my trousers and my cap.

"How seriously wounded?" I had to ask.

The army man let Thomas answer. "I don't think I'm going to make it, Polly."

"You have to make it!"

The army man pulled me away. "That's not for us to decide, miss. That's up to God."

14

Still grieving for Polly, Amanda forced her-self to go back to the kitchen.

"Steffi!" their mother called loudly.

Steffi appeared in the kitchen doorway. "What are we having?"

"Spaghetti. I know it's not your favorite, but everyone's going to eat it without complaining. Get Peanut her wet food."

"Why can't Amanda do it?"

"Amanda just got home. She had a narrow escape on her bike."

"No kidding!" Steffi looked interested. "A car? How much did it miss you by?"

"Steffi!"

"Well, it *didn't* hit her." From the cupboard Steffi took out the small china saucer on which they put a heaping spoonful of wet food for Peanut every night. Usually at the clink of the dish, Peanut came running into the kitchen, meowing with eagerness for the first bite.

"Where's Peanut?" Steffi asked.

"She's around here somewhere."

"Peanut! Dinner!"

Even the whir of the electric can opener, Peanut's favorite sound in the whole world, didn't produce her.

"Maybe she ate a mouse, and she's full?" Steffi suggested.

Their mother turned off the burner under the spaghetti sauce. "She's probably behind a door somewhere. Girls, go look for her."

Amanda followed Steffi out of the kitchen.

"You look upstairs, and I'll look downstairs," Steffi said.

Amanda walked through every bedroom and opened every closet door, but no little cat was trapped anywhere. Her father's closet wasn't empty anymore. Her mother had moved her summer clothes into it. Gone was the framed wedding picture that had once stood on their bureau. Amanda wondered if their mother had just put it away, or if she had ripped it into a thousand tiny pieces and dumped it in the trash.

"I hope she didn't get outside," their mother said when both girls returned to the kitchen. "I didn't have the back door latched before, and the wind blew it open."

Amanda's heart clenched within her. Peanut never went outside. She wouldn't know how dangerous cars were, or foxes, or hostile cats.

Without a word, Amanda and Steffi both headed out into the yard.

"Take your jackets, girls!" their mother called.

The door banged shut behind them.

Bad things always come in threes, Amanda had heard it said. The scene with Lance and James was the first bad thing; seeing her father at the Arts Center was the second bad thing; now, if Peanut was gone forever, that would be the third bad thing. She had visions of biking through the neighborhood, tacking up signs on every lamppost: LOST CAT. ORANGE WITH TAN STRIPES. VERY SOFT AND CUDDLY AND AFFECTIONATE. THE SWEETEST CAT IN THE WHOLE WIDE WORLD.

Anxiously, Amanda peered into the darkness for a glimpse of light-colored fur, or a pair of glowing green eyes. Beth wouldn't even be helping her put up the signs, because Beth would be too busy Irish dancing with Meghan. Maybe losing Beth was the first bad thing. Then she'd have three bad things already, and Peanut would be found.

"Do you think bad things come in threes?" she asked Steffi as they circled the yard, crouching to look under each bordering bush. A small animal darted across the grass, but it was a squirrel, not a cat.

"No, bad things just come. I guess people say they come in threes because after they get three bad things, they stop counting. By that point, it's just all bad."

It wasn't a comforting answer.

"Peanut!" Amanda called. "Peanut!"

"I have an idea," Steffi said. "I'll run back inside and get a plate and spoon and tap against it."

She took longer than Amanda expected.

"I brought two plates. When they clink against each other—that's the sound she likes. Oh, and I called Ben to see if he had any other ideas. He said cats who aren't used to going outside can get so frightened and overwhelmed that they just freeze. He said they usually don't go very far."

Several times Steffi clinked the plates and tapped the spoon against them. "Peanut! Wet food!"

If Peanut hadn't gone very far, where was she? "Maybe she got hit by a car," Amanda said dully.

Steffi gave her shoulder an angry poke. "Let's look on the bright side, why don't we? You have car accidents on the brain tonight."

But Steffi led the way to the front of the house. Amanda could hardly bear to look at the road, for fear of seeing a small furry body lying there. When she did look, the pavement was bare under the circle of brightness from the streetlamp.

"What was your second bad thing?" Steffi asked. "Your almost bike accident, and what else?"

Amanda was surprised that Steffi had figured out why she had asked the question.

"I didn't really have an almost accident." She paused, to let Steffi know that what she had to say next was important. "I saw her."

"Who?"

"Her."

Steffi dropped down on the curb. Amanda sat beside her, their shoulders touching. Dead leaves had drifted against the concrete, where the wind had blown them.

"She was just like you said she would be." Amanda picked up a leaf and crumbled it between her fingers. "Long blond hair. Lipstick. Everything."

"Where did you see her? Are you sure it was really *her*?"

"I was at the Arts Center after school, and I saw him coming out of a sax lesson—"

"He doesn't take sax lessons."

"He does now. And she was there to meet him."

"How old did she look?"

"I don't know. Younger than Mom."

"Was she pretty?"

"I guess so. In sort of a fancy way. Steffi . . ." Amanda could hardly get the words out. "He kissed her."

"On the cheek? Or on the lips?"

Amanda didn't even bother to reply.

"Did you say anything to Mom?"

"No! But—she knows, doesn't she? I mean, that would explain why . . ."

"People usually know." Amanda waited to see if Steffi would tell her about different movie stars and how they found out that their husbands or wives were involved with other movie stars. Maybe they read it in the fan magazines, just like everybody else. But all Steffi said was, "Mom knows."

Amanda felt something brush against her leg and heard a piteous meow.

"Peanut!" She snatched the cat up and cuddled her. "Oh, Peanut Butter!"

Steffi reached over and petted Peanut's head and stroked her small, quivering nose.

Peanut tried to wriggle out of Amanda's arms, but Amanda held her close as the two girls silently went back inside to the welcoming warmth and light of the kitchen.

"There she is!" Their mother's voice was full of relief; she must have been more worried about Peanut than she had let on. "Steffi, Ben called while you two were outside looking. He said to call him back as soon as you found her, even if it was late. Go ahead, call him now. The spaghetti might as well wait a little bit longer."

This time Steffi didn't take the phone upstairs; she stood by the stove, punching Ben's number in by memory.

"Hi, Ben, it's Steffi. We found her!" The story came pouring out, punctuated by pauses where Ben must have been saying, "Uh-huh," or "That's great." Amanda couldn't tell if Steffi was happier that Peanut was found or that she had an excuse for talking to Ben.

There was a longer pause on Steffi's side of the conversation.

"Sure!" Steffi said. "Anytime."

She mouthed to Amanda, "He wants to come by and see Peanut!"

"After your game on Saturday? That would be great. I'm planning to go."

Steffi was beaming when she came to the table. Their mother set a filled plate of spaghetti in front of her.

"I love spaghetti!" Steffi said. She gazed down at her plate with a smile of rapturous appreciation. Amanda knew it wasn't spaghetti that Steffi was so thrilled about.

"Steffi," their mother said in a low, serious voice.

"What?" Steffi already had her mouth full.

"Ben is in high school, honey."

Steffi gulped down her spaghetti. "I know that. I'm the one who told you he was in high school."

"It's just that . . . maybe Ben is being nice, taking such an interest in Peanut and how she's adjusting, worrying with us when we thought she was lost."

"What's wrong with being nice?" Now Steffi's eyes were glittering with suspicious anger.

"There's nothing wrong with being nice. I just don't want you to read more into this than is there."

"So you don't think Ben could really like me. You don't think your own daughter is likable enough that a boy could *want* to call her on the phone and *want* her to come to his soccer game."

"I didn't say that."

"It's what you meant, though, isn't it? 'Don't read more into this than is there.' Just because you're not nice, you think it's odd when anybody's nice."

"Steffi! I can't let you talk to me like this."

But Amanda knew that once Steffi started, she was impossible to stop.

"You think nobody would want to go out with me because you're not likable enough that Dad would want to stay with you."

Steffi herself seemed to realize that she had gone too far. She shot an anguished glance at Amanda.

"Your father and I have our own reasons for separating," their mother said in a frighteningly quiet voice, "and I don't intend to discuss them with you. Steffi, I don't want you to get hurt, that's all. Am I such a terrible mother because I don't want you to get hurt?"

She was starting to cry now, and Steffi was crying, too.

"No," Steffi said between gulping sobs. "You're not a terrible mother. I shouldn't have said those things. I shouldn't have said them."

"I just don't want you to get hurt," their mother said again.

"But maybe I won't get hurt. And maybe it's worth it, getting hurt. Maybe getting hurt once in a while isn't the end of the world."

Their mother reached for a tissue, blew her nose, and then passed the tissue box to Steffi. She forced a shaky smile, and Steffi returned it.

Amanda hadn't finished her spaghetti, but she wasn't hungry anymore. She patted her lap, and Peanut jumped onto it, kneaded her sweatshirt a few times with sharp little claws, and then settled down against her chest and started to purr.

Amanda knew that Steffi was right. If Peanut had been lost forever, it would have broken her heart, but she would still have been glad to have had Peanut in her life.

And Peanut *had* been found. Amanda stroked the soft, soft fur on Peanut's neck, and Peanut kept on purring.

July 30, 1861

Dear Diary,

I told Mr. Porter I had to stay and wait to see what happened to Thomas.

"Well, Polly," he said, "do you reckon it's time to send a telegram to your folks to let them know what's been goin' on? I don't want to leave you here all alone, but I have crops to tend and a family of my own. Do you have any kin you can stay with here in the city?"

I knew he was right. "My Aunt Sally and Uncle William."

"I'll take you there, and they can take care of sending a telegram for you."

I gave him their address and climbed back into the wagon and settled into Mr. Porter's alfalfa for the last time. He had been so good to me. A complete stranger going from hospital to hospital with a scared, lonely girl dressed as a boy who was searching for one wounded brother and ended up finding two.

For the first time in a long time, I thought of Mother and Father, how worried they must be, about Jeb, about Thomas, and now about me. The world was so full of terrible things to worry about.

From the wagon I could see a woman standing in a doorway, reading a telegram. The Western Union man stood there while she opened the envelope and took out the single sheet of paper. Then she began to scream, "No! No! My Robert dead? No! No!"

She fell to her knees, sobbing and beating the ground with her bare fists.

One little piece of paper had changed her life forever.

Mr. Porter's horses kept walking. They didn't even turn their heads to see why some woman was screaming by the side of the road. But Mr. Porter turned back to look at me, and I saw that his eyes were full of tears. He didn't stop the wagon, though. There was nothing he could do for the woman. There was nothing anyone could do.

As long as I live, I'll never forget hearing her cry, "No! No!"

When we reached Aunt Sally's house, Mr. Porter lifted me down from the wagon and waited while I knocked on the front door.

Jessie Mae, Aunt Sally's cook, opened it. At first she didn't recognize me. Then I pulled off my cap.

"Why, Miss Polly! What are you doing here so far from home?"

She looked at Mr. Porter as if he would explain everything, but he said, "I'll let Polly tell you her story. I'd best be going now."

I gave him a big hug, and he hugged me back. "Oh, Mr. Porter! Thank you, thank you!"

Then he left and drove away. I didn't even have his address so that I could write to him. He had been by my side on the most important journey of my life, and now he was gone.

Aunt Sally showed up in the doorway then.

"Polly! Oh, praise God, you're safe!"

"I went to look for Jeb."

Then she was crying, and I was crying, and Jessie Mae was crying, too.

We sent a telegram home that night:

POLLY SAFE STOP JEB LOST ARM STOP THOMAS HURT BAD STOP KEEP PRAYING

15

Amanda couldn't sleep that night. She had always been good at sleeping. Next to writing, it was her best talent: as soon as she laid her head down on the pillow, she was swept off into a deep, dreamless slumber; if she ever tried to read for a while in bed, the book would fall out of her hand after a page or two, and the next thing she'd know, it was morning. One of her parents would have come in during the night to turn off her light. Probably her mother.

Yes, it had to have been her mother who always crept up to the bed while she was sleeping, and closed her book, and tucked the covers in around her. Of that she was suddenly sure. Not her father. Not her father, ever.

How could she have been so blind? Steffi had known before she did. That was why Steffi hadn't believed his lie about the crab sandwich. "That's what Dad *said*": Steffi had practically accused him of lying right then. But the crab sandwich story had sounded so real when he said it; he had even added extra details to make it more convincing. Amanda couldn't believe that he could lie so smoothly to his own daughter, knowing that she would believe him simply because she wanted to so desperately.

Over and over again, the scene replayed itself in Amanda's mind—waiting in the lobby, then seeing him there, then his kiss, not on her cheek, full on her lips. And the way his face looked when he saw her. His face never looked like that when he saw Amanda. For Mandy he wouldn't even take the chain off the motel door . . .

★ ★ ★

Amanda must have fallen asleep, because her mother came in to wake her at seven.

"Time to get up, honey," her mother said. "It's not like you to oversleep. That scare on your bike must have taken a lot out of you."

What scare? Oh, her lie. The lie she had told about her bike so she wouldn't have to tell the truth about her father.

"Mom?"

"What is it, honey?"

"I love you."

Her mother's eyes filled with tears. "I love you, too, Amanda. These last few weeks—"

Amanda shook her head. She didn't want her mother to

say anything more. So her mother touched her cheek gently and left her alone to get dressed for school.

At breakfast, Steffi was silent and sullen. Amanda knew Steffi was embarrassed about the night before, about the things she had said to their mother, about letting them see her cry. If she was extra nice to Steffi, it would only make things worse. Instead, Amanda brushed Peanut, who lay on the floor, stretching herself out in rapture at every stroke of the brush.

"Poor little Peanut," Amanda crooned. "You were lost, but we found you."

"She wasn't lost!" Steffi snapped. "She was there all along, probably ten feet away from us. We made a big fuss yesterday over nothing."

She glared at Amanda, as if daring her to offer any contradiction. Amanda didn't.

★ ★ ★

"Bring your diaries to the gathering place," Mr. Abrams said once the Pledge of Allegiance and morning announcements were over.

Amanda retrieved hers from her desk, but she wasn't going to read it to the class, even if they all got down on their knees and begged her. Except for James, the others didn't deserve to hear about Polly. They wouldn't understand about losing a brother. In their whole lives, they had probably never lost anything.

Well, Lance's parents were divorced, Amanda remembered. But he was the last person in the world to whom she would read her Polly entry, after what he had done to James. She wouldn't read it to Beth, either, who had made as much fun of her poor grieving widow as Lance had made of his poor ignorant slave boy.

For the first time, the diary project seemed stupid—worse than stupid, *wrong*. All these fifth graders with their easy, comfortable lives pretending to be long-ago people who had suffered the unspeakable tragedies of a terrible war. And then sitting in a circle reading aloud to one another and giggling.

"I think it's time to hear from our heads of state," Mr. Abrams said. He called on a boy named Scott, who was doing Jefferson Davis, the President of the Confederacy.

Jefferson Davis was having a bad time. He had counted on England to come to the aid of the Confederacy, because English aristocrats had a lot in common with Southern plantation owners, and England didn't like equality any more than the South did. But England wasn't helping the South. Queen Victoria had read *Uncle Tom's Cabin* and cried at what happened to the slaves in the story.

"I can't believe one made-up story could make such a big difference," Scott had Jefferson Davis say.

Amanda could believe it. She knew that Abraham Lincoln had told Harriet Beecher Stowe, the author of *Uncle Tom's*

Cabin, "So this is the little lady who wrote the book that made this great war."

Ricky, as President Lincoln, read next.

" 'Today I freed the slaves. I wrote something called the Emancipation Proclamation. I don't know why I called it that. But even if it has a confusing name, it freed all the slaves in the South. They should have been free a long time ago. But I'm glad they're free now. This is the best thing I've done as President.' "

The class clapped at the end of Ricky's journal. Amanda knew they weren't clapping for Ricky as much as for President Lincoln. But maybe they were clapping for Ricky, as well. Amanda had gotten a strange little thrill when Ricky read the last line of his diary. For some reason it made her like Ricky more than she had before.

"Who wants to read next?" Mr. Abrams asked. As usual, Lance waved his hand in the air. Before calling on him, Mr. Abrams ran his eyes around the circle as if to see if there was anyone else he could call on instead. Amanda almost raised her hand, just so that she wouldn't have to hear Lance read, but she didn't.

"Okay, Lance." If Mr. Abrams was disappointed at having to hear yet another Jonah entry, he didn't show it.

"Mine is about the Emancipation Proclamation, too," Lance said. " 'Dear Diary'—*d-e-r-e* Diary—"

"You can let us imagine the spelling," Mr. Abrams suggested.

" 'Today I's heard that Massah Lincoln—he's de President—he make sumpin' called de—Eman—Eman—Eman—I's can't say such a big word. But it means I's free. 'Cept my missus, she don't listen to Massah Lincoln. She says I's not free. I's not sure I want to be free. My massah and missus whip me, but dey feed me, too. How's I feed myself if I free? I can't eat cotton. Mebbe dis Eman—Eman—Eman is not such a good idea.' The end."

"Comments for Lance?" Mr. Abrams asked in his usual level voice.

No one said anything. Even Ricky didn't say he liked everything about it. How could he, after he had been the one to free the slaves?

Suddenly Amanda heard herself speaking.

"Is it supposed to be *funny* that he can't say the words *Emancipation Proclamation*? Are we supposed to be *laughing*? Jonah is a *slave*. He's never been to school. He picks cotton all day long and gets whipped for not picking it faster. How is he supposed to be able to say the words *Emancipation Proclamation*?"

"Amanda, our rule is to start with something positive," Mr. Abrams reminded her gently.

"Positive? *Positive?* There's nothing positive! All Lance has done in every single journal entry is make fun of Jonah. That's all he's done. And now—he says Jonah doesn't want to be free? Jonah wants to stay a slave? If Lance had thought about Jonah's feelings for even one second, he'd know that's not true. Nobody could want to be a slave. If Lance doesn't know that, he doesn't know anything!"

Amanda couldn't stay in the room another minute, or she'd grab Lance's diary out of his hands and rip it into little pieces and hurl them in his smug, smiling face. She leaped to her feet and ran out of the room and stood in the hallway, her heart racing and her shoulders shaking.

Mr. Abrams found her there a moment later, his kindly face creased with lines of concern. "Amanda, what's all this about? I know Lance's diary hasn't been as sensitively written as it could have been, but you're so upset, and I think you've hurt Lance's feelings, and hurt them badly."

"He hurt James's feelings!"

Mr. Abrams seemed surprised. "Are you sure that's true? James seems to me to be a very grounded and secure young man. I doubt he's taking Lance's diary personally."

"Yesterday? After the audition results were posted? James got picked, and Lance didn't, and Lance called James"—she forced out the word—"Jonah."

Mr. Abrams covered his eyes. Then he put his hand on Amanda's shoulder. "Thank you for telling me," he said. "That explains a lot."

Amanda felt relieved that Mr. Abrams knew. "What are you going to do?"

"Talk to Lance. Talk to James. I knew there was a risk, with this kind of assignment. But there's a greater risk if we don't at least try to understand someone else's experience from the inside. And sometimes—sometimes the results are pretty wonderful. Your Polly diary, for example. When you read aloud, I almost feel you *are* Polly."

"I almost feel I'm Polly, too."

Mr. Abrams patted Amanda's shoulder. "Let's go do some math," he said.

Amanda followed him back to the room. A few kids shot curious looks in her direction, but most had their heads bent over their math worksheets. Right then, Amanda was grateful for the existence of fractions and decimals. Right then, they seemed less complicated than dealing with human beings in the Civil War, and human beings in the here and now.

August 1, 1861

Dear Diary,

Mother and Father arrived at Aunt Sally's today. I was afraid to see them. I knew they had to be very angry. But Mother just hugged me, and Father hugged me, too, though he is not one for showing his feelings.

Later Mother did say, "What if your Mr. Porter hadn't been an honorable man?"

And Father said, "Didn't you think your mother and I had enough to worry about with both boys off to war?"

Then I cried, and Mother cried, and Father didn't cry, but he blew his nose on his checkered handkerchief extra hard.

Now we are going in Aunt Sally's buggy to the hospital to see Thomas.

If Thomas is still here. "I don't think I'm going to make it, Polly." *Those were his last words to me.*

★ ★ ★

We're at the hospital, dear Diary. I brought you with me so I can write to you while Mother and Father go inside and find out. They told me to wait here. They don't think an army hospital is a proper place for a young lady. I told them I'd been to two hospitals already. Still, they left me here, sitting underneath this tree.

I'll know by their faces when they come out. Well, I'll know the news is bad if Father is crying. Mother will cry either way. Every time someone comes out of the hospital, I look up, thinking it's them. But it never is.

I'm starting to hope. Would they be taking so long if Thomas were dead?

Unless they had to arrange for what to do with his body and get the flag, all folded in a special way, that would cover his coffin. If they give out flags like that during a war.

Maybe there aren't enough flags in the world to cover all the coffins of all the boys killed in all the wars.

Wait. It's them. They're coming.

16

It had been two days since Amanda had talked to her dad during his nightly phone call. She had made sure to be in the shower at eight o'clock the night that Peanut was lost and found; Friday night she was at the library reading more about the Civil War.

On Saturday, Steffi and Tanya went to Ben's game. Amanda kept looking at her watch while Steffi was gone, wondering if the game was almost over, wondering if Ben would really come back to their house afterward to see Peanut. She caught her mother checking the clock a few times, too.

At one-thirty, she heard Steffi's voice in the kitchen, and then a boy's voice responding. She didn't hear Tanya's voice; Tanya must have obligingly disappeared after the game.

Should she stay in her room or go downstairs to say hi to Ben herself? Well, Peanut was on her bed, so if Ben was going to see Peanut, she'd have to carry her down for his inspection.

"There she is!" Ben said as Amanda shyly came into the kitchen with Peanut in her arms. In his soccer uniform, Ben looked even cuter, and Steffi looked even more smitten.

Ben took Peanut from Amanda. The cat let him pet her, instead of struggling to jump down.

"She looks great!" Ben said. "I think she's gained a little weight. That's good—she was pretty skinny—but you probably don't want her to gain any more. How much are you feeding her?"

Their mother appeared in the kitchen; Amanda could tell she was trying to make it look as if she had just felt the need for another cup of coffee.

"Ben!" She tried to act surprised to see him. "How nice of you to stop by."

"Well, I wanted to see Peanut," Ben said. "And Steffi," he added, blushing as he said it. Amanda had never seen a boy blush before, or maybe she had just never noticed.

Amanda and her mother exchanged a quick glance. Amanda knew her mother had never been more grateful to have been wrong about something.

"Would you like a snack?" their mother asked. "We have plenty of fixings for sandwiches."

"That'd be great."

"*I* can make him a sandwich," Steffi said. It was clearly

the signal to go. Steffi flashed her mother and sister a joyous smile as they went.

★ ★ ★

Then it was Sunday, and Amanda and Steffi were supposed to go visit their dad at Georgetown Meadows.

"I don't want to go," Amanda told Steffi.

"Like what we want matters?"

"He's going to know that we know."

"So? We were bound to find out sometime. Maybe he'll sit us down and tell us about her, and we can act surprised. Or maybe he'll want us to meet her, and she'll be desperate for us to like her, and she'll buy us all kinds of stuff that Mom won't let us have."

When their dad came right on time to collect them, both sisters walked silently to the car. It was a perfect sunny afternoon. The maple leaves were an intense scarlet against the dazzling blueness of the October sky.

Like blood, Amanda thought. That's what they would look like to Polly—leaves drenched with blood freshly shed by her wounded brothers.

"Pretty day," their father remarked.

Neither girl replied.

Their dad's apartment looked lived in now, with a heap of newspapers strewn on the coffee table, and his laptop and printer set up on the dining room table with a bunch of cords trailing down to the floor. Their mother's printer had jammed again the other night, and she had actually found the owner's manual that came with it and unjammed it herself.

On the couch lay his saxophone. Steffi nudged Amanda and angled her chin toward it. Amanda couldn't believe he would leave it there in full view for them to see. Quickly she averted her eyes.

He had already seen their reaction to it.

"I've been taking sax lessons," he said. As if to prove it, he picked up the sax and played a couple of scales.

"Your mother never liked the sound of the sax. Or, I should say, the sound of my playing on the sax. Not that I could blame her. I've heard dying cats that sounded better. But I figured—now that—"

Breaking off the sentence, he shrugged apologetically.

I know you're taking sax lessons. I saw you at the Arts Center on Thursday.

"Okay!" he said cheerfully, laying the sax back down on the couch. "What do you girls want to do this afternoon? I thought of some ideas. Let's not just spend our time together watching TV."

Steffi had already clicked the remote to the Food Network. "What's wrong with TV?"

He produced a piece of paper from his pocket. "Idea number one, go to the crafts festival at the county fairgrounds, right outside of town. Idea number two, go for a short hike to see the autumn foliage. Idea number three, go to a free folk music concert at the public library."

"Idea number four, stay here and watch TV," Steffi said.

To Amanda, all three of their dad's ideas sounded like fun, especially the crafts festival. That he had actually written them down made her have to fight the familiar pang of pity for him. People who said, "If at first you don't succeed, try, try, try again," didn't know how *sad* trying could be. But she hadn't forgotten the way his face had shone when he had seen the blond lady at the Arts Center. He could take *her* to the crafts festival, on the hike, to the concert.

"Mandy?"

She made herself say it. "I vote for idea number four." She plopped herself on the couch beside Steffi, wishing that her dad would put the saxophone away, someplace where she and Steffi wouldn't have to see it.

"Suit yourselves," he said shortly. Out of the corner of her eye, Amanda saw him sit down at the dining room table and start typing on his laptop. E-mailing *her*, probably.

Amanda caught him looking at her with a hurt, puzzled expression.

She fixed her eyes back on the TV.

★ ★ ★

The Civil War concert was held on Wednesday night; the class trip to Gettysburg would follow on Friday. Amanda's mother and Steffi were going to the concert, but not her father. She hadn't told him about it at the Sunday visit, or during any of the brief, awkward conversations that followed, even though he had asked her, flat out, "Any school programs coming up?"

She had said no.

But now that it was the night of the concert, Amanda thought her heart would break, not having him there. He had never missed a school concert or play for her or Steffi, ever. He was always there in the front row with his video camera and proud grin, acting as if a kindergarten Thanksgiving play was the most wonderful thing in the world if his daughter was the third Pilgrim from the left, the one whose Pilgrim hat kept slipping down over her eyes. He'd even give her flowers afterward, making her feel like a movie star.

She almost called him from school half an hour before the concert. There was still time for him to get there, even though it was too late for him to claim his favorite front-row seat.

But she didn't call him.

Mrs. Angelino had told the fifth graders to try to look as much like Civil War children as possible. Most of the boys had on jeans and flannel shirts; the girls wore cotton dresses, if they had them. A few girls, including Amanda, wore sunbonnets. Amanda's father had bought her a sunbonnet at a crafts fair once, because he knew how much she loved old-fashioned things. Beth and Meghan had on their matching

Irish dancing costumes, complete with matching curly wigs. With their wigs on, you could hardly tell them apart.

The fifth graders were lined up outside, ready to march into the gym and up onto the stage to sing their opening number, "Dixie." Standing there, through the windows, they could see their families seated in the rows of folding chairs set up for the occasion.

Beth was behind Amanda in line. "Where's your dad?" she asked. "I see your mom and Steffi, but I don't see your dad."

The casual innocence of the question was too much.

"Oh, he left," Amanda said airily.

"Left? Like on a business trip?"

"No, *left*. Moved out. Got his own apartment. Ages ago. My parents are separated. Didn't you know?"

From the gym came the opening strains of "Dixie," pounded out by Mrs. Angelino on the battered old upright piano below the front edge of the stage. It was the fifth graders' signal to begin marching in.

Amanda whirled away from Beth's shocked face and stepped briskly in time to the rousing beat of the tune. When the fifth graders were all assembled on the risers, Mrs. Angelino mouthed to them, "Smile!"

Amanda's smile was the biggest and brightest.

"Oh, I wish I was in the land of cotton!"

Ninety fifth-grade students picked their cotton. Appreciative laughter came often from the audience. Even though Mrs. Angelino took her choreographed motions very seriously, the parents always thought they were funny.

"Look away! Look away! Look away! Dixie Land!"

Finally the song was over. At a sign from Mrs. Angelino, they all sat down in place on the risers.

"Welcome to our Civil War concert!" Mrs. Angelino said into the microphone. "Our fifth-grade boys and girls have worked *very hard* to prepare for you a special program of song, dance, and poetry!"

Amanda felt Beth poke her with her elbow. "Why didn't you tell me?" Beth whispered.

"How could I tell you?" Amanda whispered back. "You were always busy with your new best friend, doing Irish jigs."

The audience applauded. Mrs. Angelino must have finished her welcoming speech. A fifth grader from another class came to the center of the stage with her violin.

"That's not fair!" Beth whispered as the girl began to play some tune Amanda didn't recognize. "You're the one who was acting strange, never calling me, never inviting me to your house anymore."

Mrs. Angelino shot them a warning look, the kind she usually reserved for Lance and Ricky.

Amanda saved her reply until the girl played the last refrain of her piece. "You didn't even ask me what was wrong!

We've been best friends for how many years? Five? And you didn't even *ask*!"

"Maybe I thought I didn't *have* to ask, that if something was wrong, you'd *tell* me."

Mrs. Angelino signaled for the fifth graders to stand up again. Amanda and Beth rose with the others.

"Our next song is about the favorite snack of the Confederate soldiers. Parents, see if you can guess what *goober peas* are. Or ask your fifth grader!"

Amanda was so upset she could hardly get the words out. She wished she and Beth weren't standing smack in the center of the front row, instead of safely in the back with the klutzy kids like Patrick, who always messed up the motions. It was hideous to have to turn to Beth and merrily pantomime, "Chatting with my messmates." Having the worst fight of your life with your ex-best friend was more like it.

"Peas, peas, peas, peas, Eatin' goober peas! Goodness, how delicious, Eatin' goober peas!"

Amanda vowed never to eat a peanut again.

A very short fifth-grade boy read a poem. Even with the microphone, he was hard to hear. Another boy played the trumpet.

All together, the fifth graders sang "My Old Kentucky Home." The parents didn't laugh at the motions for that one— big circled arms for "The sun shines bright in the old Kentucky home"; eyes wiped for "Weep no more, my lady." The music was too sad and yearning, sighing for a home far away.

Like a father far away.

Like a best friend lost forever.

Amanda whispered just one line to Beth during the applause for "My Old Kentucky Home."

"You shouldn't have to *tell* best friends things. They should *know*."

"Maybe I'm not a mind reader," Beth whispered back.

Amanda hated to admit that Beth might have a point.

Mrs. Angelino took the microphone again. "Next we'll have an Irish jig by our two wonderful Irish dancers, Beth Gibson and Meghan Moore."

Beth shot Amanda one furious glance and then joined Meghan in the spotlight. Mrs. Angelino turned on the CD of their music, and the two girls began to dance. Amanda could see Beth only from the back, but she was sure Beth was smiling her big, fixed Irish-dancing smile that exactly matched Meghan's big, fixed Irish-dancing smile. Their feet clattered in perfect unison.

The applause afterward was the loudest yet.

"And now Amanda MacLeish will share with us her original poem 'Polly's Lament.' "

She couldn't do it. But Mrs. Angelino turned toward her expectantly, so Amanda had no choice but to come forward to the microphone.

"Polly's Lament," she repeated into the mike.

How did it go? She should have written it down on a piece of paper, just in case, but she never would have imagined that she could forget her own poem that was only ten lines long. She had also never imagined that she'd be fighting bitterly with Beth through the entire Civil War concert. Or that her father wouldn't be there to see her perform.

"Polly's Lament," she said again.

It was just as well that her father wasn't videotaping this one. She stood there for what felt like hours in appalled, terrified silence.

Then, from behind her, she heard Beth's soft voice: "My brother Jeb fights for the South."

Amanda recited:

"My brother Jeb fights for the South.
My brother Thomas, for the North.
I do not fight for either side.
I watch the soldiers marching forth."

One line followed another, effortlessly now, and the poem came to a close. Amanda didn't acknowledge the applause. She fled back to her spot next to Beth.

She had to thank Beth, but she didn't trust herself to speak. She reached over and squeezed Beth's hand.

Beth squeezed hers back.

Then it was James's turn. If "My Old Kentucky Home" was sad, James's violin solo was even sadder. As James played,

Amanda blinked back tears. Next to her, she could hear Beth sniffle.

Beth wasn't the one who had betrayed the friendship by not asking; Amanda had betrayed it, by not telling. But it had been so hard to tell Beth, when her family was happy and Amanda's was miserable. Still, Beth couldn't help having a happy family. And Amanda *had* tried to tell Beth, though she hadn't tried very hard.

A tear trickled down Amanda's cheek. She wiped it away.

The applause for James was the evening's loudest. Even Lance was clapping. She didn't know what Mr. Abrams had said to Lance and James, but Lance was definitely clapping for James now.

"I'm sorry," Amanda whispered to Beth as they both kept on clapping for James.

"I'm sorry, too."

They gave each other one brief, fierce hug.

For the concert finale, all the fifth graders sang "The Battle Hymn of the Republic." Fortunately, Mrs. Angelino didn't have them do motions for this song. They just stood there and belted it out. "Glory, glory, hallelujah! Glory, glory, hallelujah!" You didn't need motions when you had words like that to sing.

Amanda's joy at singing with Beth beside her warred with the pain of missing her father.

"Glory, glory, hallelujah!" she sang, her heart filled to overflowing.

Dear Diary,

He's alive!

He lost a leg, his right leg, but he's alive.

He's going to come home with us in three more days. The army has no use for a one-legged soldier.

I remember how sad I was when I learned that Jeb had lost his arm. Losing a leg is even worse than losing an arm, but I can't be sad this time. Losing a leg is so much better than losing your whole life.

"I don't think I'm going to make it, Polly."

But he did make it! He did!

Glory, glory, hallelujah!

He'll be coming home—home to Mother and Father and Shep and Whitie and Blackie and me.

But he won't be coming home to Jeb. Jeb's still away at the war. And even when Jeb does come home, how can Jeb forgive Thomas for fighting for the army that cost him his arm? How can Thomas ever forgive Jeb for fighting for the army that took his leg?

And how can I ever forgive both of them for fighting each other?

17

It rained on Friday, the day of the class trip to Gettysburg. At first Amanda was disappointed when she woke up to hear the rain against her window—not a gentle, misting drizzle but a hard, driving downpour. But maybe miserable weather was more fitting for a trip to the battlefield where over fifty thousand men had fallen.

"Aren't you lucky," Steffi said at breakfast. "You get to ride on a bus for an hour and then get soaked trudging through this big, boring field in the rain, and then ride on a bus again for another hour."

"I wish I could go," their mother said. Steffi gave a snort of laughter.

"I'm serious! Mr. Abrams e-mailed all the parents yesterday that he still needs more parent volunteers, but I already had plans to show three houses today."

"I bet a lot of parents *made* other plans real fast," Steffi said.

"Amanda, you'd better wear your boots. The field might be muddy. With boots, and your raincoat, and your umbrella, I think you'll be okay. I heard that it's supposed to rain all day."

As she dropped Amanda off at school, her mother reached across the front seat to kiss her. They didn't kiss goodbye on regular school mornings. The kiss made Amanda feel that she was setting off on a real journey.

In their classroom, Mr. Abrams called everyone over to the gathering place for final instructions.

"You may choose your seatmate for the bus," he told them.

Amanda and Beth and Meghan had already decided to sit together—Amanda and Beth in one seat and Meghan across the aisle on the way there, Meghan and Beth in one seat and Amanda across the aisle on the way back. Lance and Ricky would be sitting together, of course. James usually partnered with Scott, the boy who was Jefferson Davis.

"Now, remember, we are visiting a battlefield, not a theme park. In the Gettysburg Address, President Lincoln said, 'We can not dedicate—we can not consecrate—we can not hallow this ground. The brave men, living and dead, who struggled here, have consecrated it, far above our poor power to add or detract.' What does that mean?"

James raised his hand partway, then put it down again.

Mr. Abrams smiled at him. "James?"

"He means, it's sacred ground because so many soldiers died there."

"That's right, James. Let's respect that, okay, kids? With behavior that honors their sacrifice."

Amanda was impressed that he managed not to look at Lance and Ricky as he said it.

"Parent volunteers." He turned to the parents who were gathering in the back of the room. "Thank you so much for taking time out of your busy schedules to accompany us today. Kids, please give your parents a hand."

Amanda turned to see which parents were coming on the trip. She saw Beth's mother, and Ricky's mother, and a few other moms.

Then she saw her father.

She had never told him the date of the trip. He must have found out from Mr. Abrams's e-mail.

He gave her a tentative, hopeful smile.

She didn't smile back.

The bus was parked in the school parking lot, on the edge of a huge, spreading puddle that was fast becoming a small lake. Lance and Ricky stomped through it, sending up tidal waves of spray.

"Ricky!" his mother yelled.

Ricky didn't respond.

"Ricky," Mr. Abrams said quietly.

Ricky stopped. His mother looked stunned. Amanda

thought she must be trying to figure out how Mr. Abrams did it.

The parents all sat together toward the front of the bus. Amanda, Beth, and Meghan chose seats halfway back.

"Your father's here," Beth whispered to Amanda. "Did you know he was coming?"

Amanda shook her head. She had told Beth about everything now—everything except her dad's new girlfriend. That was just for Amanda and Steffi to share.

"Is it okay that he's here?"

"I guess so." In a way, she was glad he still cared enough to come. But if it meant that much to him to be a part of her life, why had he left? Didn't that mean he loved the blond, lipsticked woman more than he loved her?

As Steffi had warned, the bus ride was long. But, of course, it was much faster to travel by bus than by Mr. Porter's horse-drawn wagon. The soldiers would have come to Gettysburg on foot, walking every step of the way in the humid July heat. They had no raincoats or umbrellas to shield them from drenching rain. At least, Amanda didn't think they did. From what she had read, many of them didn't even have shoes.

At last they reached Gettysburg and filed into the Visitor Center at the park, to use the restrooms, see a short film, and view the elaborate Electric Map that re-created the three days of the battle. During the film, Amanda's father sat next to Beth's mother, three rows in front of where Amanda was sitting; as the auditorium darkened, they were deep in conversation. Amanda wondered if he was telling her that he had moved out. Beth's mother probably knew already, from Beth, but it would still be shocking to hear the news directly from his lips. Would he sound sad as he said it? Or relieved?

Instead of a picnic outside on the grass, they ate their sack lunches on the bus. Amanda could imagine Steffi's commentary: "So first you rode on the bus for an hour in the rain, and then you ate your lunch on the bus in the rain, and then you rode home for an hour in the rain. Fun!" Amanda left her peanut butter sandwich unfinished and gave her apple slices to Meghan.

After lunch, the class gathered in the Visitor Center to get organized for their tour of the battlefield. Amanda found herself standing next to James. They hadn't spoken since the day she had her outburst in class.

"Hey," James said, his voice as friendly as it had always been. "How's it going?"

"Okay." She knew he didn't really want to know; it was just a thing to say.

There was an awkward pause. Then James started in. "About Lance? His diary didn't really bother me. When he called me the name—that bothered me. But the diary—I know he's not the only person who thinks of black people that way, you know, as not so smart. I try not to let it get to me."

But it had to get to him, Amanda knew. Unless he really meant what he was saying? With a start, Amanda realized that she had always thought of James as black first, and as a smart person and a good writer and a great math student second. She was always being extra careful of what she said to him because he was black. In a way, that was just as racist as Lance's not being careful enough.

"Nobody could think you're not smart," Amanda said.

James shrugged.

"Especially in math. I thought nothing could be worse than fractions, and then we started decimals."

James laughed. "I like how you made your Polly hate math, too."

"And poor Polly doesn't have you to call for homework help."

James laughed again, and Amanda laughed with him.

The last straggling group came out of the restrooms, and Mr. Abrams started his explanation of their battlefield tour. They were free to wander on their own in small groups of six students led by one of the parent volunteers. Amanda was hoping her father would be assigned to another group, but when Mr. Abrams read off the names, the two of them were together: all the parents had been placed in the same groups as their children. But if a father didn't care enough about his daughter to live in the same house with her, why should he get to be in her group on a class trip?

The rain had let up a bit; the gray skies overhead were stretched somewhat thinner, like the worn heels of a pair of old woolen socks. Amanda walked more slowly than the rest of her group, partly to avoid her father, partly to be by herself for a little while, so she could enter quietly into Polly's world and see Gettysburg through Polly's eyes.

The battlefield was actually beautiful—rolling Pennsylvania farmland, the grass green even in late October, the trees still decked in their brilliant autumn colors. It was hard to picture these calm, quiet fields filled with the deafening explosions of cannon fire and the screams of wounded men and frightened horses.

Her father fell into step beside her.

Returned now to the present, Amanda could hear snippets of conversation from the group of girls ahead: "And then he goes . . ." "No kidding!" "And then I go . . ."

For a while she and her father walked along in silence.

"It's different from how I thought it would be," Amanda finally said.

"More peaceful?"

"Uh-huh. And prettier. I didn't expect a battlefield to be pretty."

"There's not much that's pretty about war."

A pair of birds, perched on the split-rail fence behind them, flew away. Amanda saw a flash of scarlet as they went by.

"Red-winged blackbirds," her father said.

They kept on walking.

"You didn't tell me you were having a concert," he said. "It was last Wednesday?"

Amanda nodded. Mr. Abrams must have made some reference to it in his e-mail.

"I asked you if you had any concerts coming up, and you said no."

Steffi would have said, "So I lied." Amanda said nothing. Her father was a fine one to talk about lying.

They had reached the shelter of a group of oak trees. Their leaves weren't bright yellow or orange or red, just a dull, depressing brown.

"You know I would have come," he went on.

Amanda glared at him. What made him think she wanted him to be there? He didn't deserve to be there; he didn't deserve to be here; he didn't deserve to be her father anymore.

"I saw you," she said, emphasizing every word.

"What?"

"At the Arts Center. I biked there to tell something to James—he's this boy in my class—and you were coming out of your sax lesson, and *she* was there, and you *kissed* her."

With some grim satisfaction, she saw him wince. With pain? With shame?

"Oh, Mandy, oh, honey."

He tried to put his arm around her shoulders. She pushed him away.

"Does Mom know? Is that why you left? Were you ever going to tell us? All this time—all this time I was thinking it was Mom's fault, and then I saw you with *her*."

"I'm sorry. Mandy, I should have said something to you

and Steffi. I didn't want you to find out like this. I had no idea you'd be at the Arts Center that day."

"What's her name?"

"Caroline."

She was that much more real, having a name.

"And, yes, your mother knows. But I didn't start seeing Caroline—seeing her that way—until after your mother and I agreed that we should separate."

"So it was your fault, not Mom's."

"It's more complicated than that."

"You kissed her! And that morning, in the motel—you lied to me. You told me that whole story about the crab sandwich, and I believed you. Steffi didn't, but I did. I never guessed—I would never have guessed—that you could lie to me."

Her father's face flushed crimson. "I was wrong, Mandy. I was very wrong. I just didn't want to hurt you. And I thought it would hurt you more if I told you the truth."

Amanda refused to let her heart soften. She wished she could close her ears as he kept on talking.

"I'm not sure about much of anything these days, but one thing I know is that when people quarrel, there's usually plenty of fault, if that's the word you want to use, to go around. I don't know of any divorce where one person was one hundred percent right, and the other person was one hundred percent wrong."

Divorce. He hadn't said *separation.*

"So you love . . . Caroline . . . more than you love Mom?"

He waited to answer for a moment. "I laugh more with Caroline, because Caroline laughs more. Caroline certainly likes *me* more than your mother does. If I played Monopoly with Caroline, we'd actually have fun playing it. There's a part of me that will always love your mother, and it's killing me to have to say that it's over, but we can't live together anymore. We just can't."

The other kids in their group had turned around and were heading back toward them. Mr. Abrams must have given the signal to return to the bus for the long ride home.

"The other thing I'm sure about?" Amanda's father said. He stopped walking, so Amanda stopped, too. "Surer than I am of anything in the world, is that I love you and Steffi. I always have, and I always will."

The slight quaver in his voice was too much for Amanda. Maybe her father was wrong, and her mother was right, or maybe they were both wrong, and neither was right, or maybe it didn't even matter who was wrong and who was right. Her parents had separated, but they were both still a part of Amanda's family. She wasn't ready to let her father go out of her life forever.

In a small voice, she said, "I love you, too, Daddy."

When he reached out to hug her this time, she let him, their two umbrellas colliding. Amanda couldn't tell if her face was more wet from the Gettysburg rain or from her own tears. She turned her face up toward him and saw that he was crying, too.

From half the field away, Beth called toward them, "Amanda! Mr. MacLeish! Mr. Abrams said it's time to go!"

"Let's go, then," Amanda's father said.

Amanda and her father walked across the silent, sacred space of the Gettysburg battlefield together.

January 10, 1862

Dear Diary,

It has been so long since I have written to you, dear Diary. The war is worse and worse and shows no sign of ending.

I am back in school again. Master Taylor is teaching us percents and decimals, and I am an even bigger dunce at them than I was at fractions. He yells at us less now, though. Ever since his son was killed at Leesburg, he doesn't have the heart to scold us about arithmetic. He doesn't even rap the knuckles of the boys who write rude things to each other on their slates.

Thomas has a peg leg that he walks on almost as fast as he walked on his real leg before. He was able to dance with Betsy's older sister, Mary, at the cornhusking bee last fall. I think they're sweet on each other.

Mother and Father are in good health, though Father's hair and beard have turned gray since the war began, and I hear Mother crying sometimes when she thinks no one is near.

Blackie still loves Thomas best, but now Whitie follows me everywhere and sits on my lap when I sew and sleeps curled up beside me on my bed. I know she will be Jeb's cat again, though, when Jeb comes home.

And, dear Diary, Jeb is coming home! He was very sick with the measles in his army camp, but now he's coming home to rest until he's well enough to fight again.

I hope his resting takes a nice long time.

He is coming home today. Mother swept the floors and baked a pie. Father brushed Nell as if a king was going to ride on her. I am knitting, knitting, knitting, trying to finish the scarf I started for Jeb in the fall. The scarf is skinnier in the middle than it is at both ends, but I don't think Jeb will mind.

Thomas can't settle down to do anything today. He keeps walking from our cabin out to the road, to peer down it to see if Jeb is coming. Then he comes inside to warm himself for a while by the stove and goes back down the road to watch some more. He's there now.

Wait—Diary—I hear him shouting.

"I see him! Ma! Pa! Polly! He's coming!"

★ ★ ★

Diary, from the window, I saw Thomas running in the crooked way he runs now on his one good leg and one wooden peg.

Jeb was running, too.

They met each other halfway. Jeb threw his only arm around

Thomas. My one-legged Union brother and one-armed Confederate brother held each other close.

Oh, Diary, there are so many different ways to be a family.

Then Mother and Father and I rushed out of the house to join in the embrace, and we all hugged each other as if we would never let go.